Please
stay with me

Petra Eggert

Impressum

Copyright © Dezember 2017 Petra Eggert Lippstadt

Copyright © Bod Verlag

Cover : © Forewer-Fotolia.com

Cover : TomJay-bookcover4everyone

9 783746 025148

www.tomjay.de

Translate : Luica Lunau

Manufactured and published by
BoD - Books on Demand, Norderstedt, Germany

Special thanks to Lucia,Tom, my Children Vivian and Benedikt and my lovely Husband. You will never forget.

Please

stay with me

Prologue

The small airplane's engines drone inexorably in my ears. The wind is blowing briskly, pulling at my head like it is trying to put my thoughts through the wringer. And it does. Here I am at the airport, my small suitcase in hand, awaiting my departure. My heart does not yet want to go home. But my head urges me on. I need to leave this place, so dreamy yet so crisp, with its endless, fleeting memories. My heart aches and my eyes fill with tears. I let them run silently down my cheeks. After all, I had wanted all of this. Hadn't I? Thinking about it, not really. Yes, I had always had the dream to go on this journey, but never quite this way, or with this result. My feelings are all over the place. Those eyes! No, Elara, don't think about him, it will only hurt you. What this is about, you ask? Of course, true to the common cliché, at the heart of the matter is a man – and an island. Ireland. Oh, what am I even saying? Let me start at the beginning.

Chapter One

My story ought to begin at the moment of fundamental change. Of course I could start out with nonsense – I was born in such-and-such, grew up in so-and-so, nurtured by my parents from x until y, fell in love, got engaged and yes, married. Divorced. Now too old and too frustrated. But no, it should not be like this. Of course the short version is entirely accurate. Sure, I could go into more detail now and talk about my marriage and its problems, but the details will come up in this story soon enough. As I said, it all begins with me sitting in front of my computer on a day like any other, doing research for a small newspaper. I had been chosen to write for them as a freelance columnist. Here and there, a small travel journal could be slipped in as well. It was sadly not going to make me rich, so I also jobbed in a supermarket. Ever since my divorce, I could only dream of distant countries. But I was not going to give up on my hopes and goals. One day, I would make the journey to Scotland, England, the USA... or Ireland. Of course this was the dream destination of every romantic, but somehow, I felt a deeper connection to the island. My heart swelled when I thought about it, and every day the longing grew stronger. My best friend Ellis, who had faithfully stood by me after the divorce, used to say: "Elara, Ireland is calling out to you. Why don't you just go?" But she knew that money was the real issue, not determination. (6)

That, I had in abundance. Anyway, the divorce marked the beginning of my life as a loner. I don't want to say that I was feeling old, but I did think that I was. I don't want to say that my relationship to my ex-husband had gotten better, but I did think he had become more approachable. Now I no longer had to listen to his constant accusations and paternalism. At the end of the day, we had simply grown apart. Now, icy silence reigned. Our interests diverged further and further. While I focused on my writing, his attention rested solely on his football club. My small newspaper column had often been target of his scorn. It wouldn't bring any money and was only read by frustrated housewives. As if. Well, I had known for a long time that divorce was the only solution. Somehow, once the decision had been made, I had felt like a weight was lifted from my chest. I finally knew, could finally escape the daily grind of marriage and the monotony of everyday life. Nobody had said it would be easy. After all, I was already well past the forty and was, in my own opinion, ready for the scrap heap. And my ex-husband could hardly believe my decision. He was convinced that I would not make it three months before crawling back to him, and that was a fact. Of course he could not have been more wrong. At this point, we had long crossed the one year mark and I had finally signed the last papers yesterday. I had to admit that I felt lighter for it, freer. Yes, there was a tinge of bitterness to it, but I was sure I   (7) would overcome it with time. Mike, my ex, walked out with downcast eyes, looking ready for the chopping block. For a change, he was the one who didn't know what to do. Well, now he had all the time in the world for his buddies. Of course they were there right away to greet him in style. Ellis had stayed by my side the entire time, and we celebrated the final signing with a ceremonial glass of champagne.

"Now you finally have time to travel," she told me. But it was not that easy. Money was forever the issue. Even though Mike called every day or even showed up at my door, wanting to help me out, as he put it. But that was the last thing I wanted. It would only end with the old status quo, minus the wedding certificate. I would be dependent on him, and he would like it a little too much. I would have to forever pretend that nothing ever happened and smooth the waves.

Today at least my day was Mike-free. He was thankfully out to see a game with his best buddy. I had to stress that he was under no circumstances to show up at my door afterward. The situation was complicated. He promised the sky and usually ended up at my door regardless, tipsy, happily reminiscing about the good old days and the glories of our oh-so-happy marriage. All the way to "how could you throw it all away", to "Let us try again". Erm, no! For me the situation was clear.

Well, after Ellis fell asleep on the sofa - she was like a guide dog, always worried about my well-being - I found myself surfing my social networks. I really ought to be researching the old city butchery, but I procrastinated. As always I got stuck on the website of my favourite band. I have to say that I was always blown away by them. I had found the band online by chance, right below a link about Ireland. They played good old folk music with Irish influences. This band was so popular that they had even made it all the way to Hollywood. I liked their music so much because it was about old myths or, typically Irish, traditional pub music. Ellis did not care for them too much, but let me be. I secretly had to admit that I quite liked the lead singer. To me he was classically Irish. Dark, wavy hair down to his shoulders, combined with grey-green eyes. Ellis always talked about Irish people being naturally small, but this was not the case for him. I felt like a teenager. It was admittedly silly to fall for some guy and his music. My friend always teased me: "Elara, what would you do if he suddenly stood in front of you?"

She then smirked a little, and I knew exactly what she was thinking.

"Oh please, Ellis, I wouldn't do anything. These things don't happen. I would maybe ask how he came to do music. But that is all."   (9)

Sometimes, I had to admit, I did dream of him. However, I knew that these dreams were based on nothing except the fact that I had been alone for a year now. That had to be the reason. Either way, Ellis slumbered after drinking a Piccolo and a long tirade on Mike. In the meantime, I had put on my headphones and was listening to the deep voice of my hero. At least this way I wouldn't hear Mike, should he knock. I did not worry about Ellis, who slept the sleep of the dead.

Night approached. Before I knew it, I was asleep on the keyboard, my headphones still on my head. I sank into the land of dreams with Kyran, the lead singer. The land of dreams was mine.

His hands stroked my hair and he pressed me close. The grin on my face was priceless. Languorously, I pressed closer. Yes, Kyran, sing for me!

"Of course, my cutie-pie," I heard his voice as if from far away. Wait a second, I wouldn't dream something like this. Especially not with him speaking to me like that. Wake up, Elara! Wake up! He demanded. What now? To wake up in the middle of my dream, oh, that was not fair. My eyelids refused to open. The other reason might be the keyboard I was glued to. What felt like five hours later I managed a glimpse   (10) and surprise, it was of course not Kyran but Ellis, who grinned at me.

"Awake, cutie-pie?" She smirked at me.

I just about managed a nod before I stretched my painfully stiff neck. Good thing that I did not need to go to work today. It would be too embarrassing to explain to my work colleagues where the G, L, B, and N imprinted on my cheek came from. My computer was still flashing, but I thought it better to turn it off.

First I had to get my face under control. A full twenty minutes later my skin was wrinkly and the letters gone. Ellis had had to go to work in the meantime, but promised to come straight back afterwards. As our holiday was approaching, we were saving up together. Big leaps were outside of our budgets. She suggested that, if I had nothing else to do for the day, I might as well check for bargains a la Mallorca or Turkey. Sun, beach and ocean were the goal. My personal tendency rather went in the direction of a north sea holiday, at a stretch the German Sauerland for three or even four days. Great! I had initially meant to muck out my flat and see what I could find for the flea market, but the weather was not in keeping with my intentions. It was raining cats and dogs, and to top it all off the phone was ringing off the hook. I could see Mike's number(11) on the display. Which to me was cause to turn up my music and ignore the permanent ringing. It went on for well over half an hour, after which I lowered my volume to the happiness of my neighbours. So far, so good, I thought and turned the computer back on. The blue flashing showed my computer was booting up. Then a "WELCOME" and my desktop loaded. Since my second boss was constantly bugging me about my newspaper column, I had to bite the bullet and check my mail first. It wouldn't do to have a final notice waiting for me. I mean, I liked the job, but to be honest, a column in a newspaper is not really a challenge for me. My email program opened, and I started to read.

"You have five new messages," it said. Beginning with "Congratulations, you have won a shopping voucher of 5€" to "Someone hacked your bank account, please verify your details by blah blah blah". Thank goodness no new message from Robert, my second boss. Maybe he had given up. When he didn't like an article, he always dug up one from ages past and pretended it was news. I quickly closed my messages and began scrolling through holiday bargains. Of course I got stuck on Ireland again. Who knew, maybe my chance would come today. Even if my hopes dwindled. To make things worse, my phone was ringing again. What would it take to shut Mike up? (12)

On second glance however, I was curious after all, I saw an unknown number. Should I answer? Whatever, probably a survey. It rang again. Fine, I thought, if I didn't answer these people just got cheekier. So I answered the phone. It crackled softly, until finally a voice became audible.

"Elara Jackson?" the voice said.

I nodded, then realised what I was doing. "Y...yes?" I asked in return. That was the signal for the voice to cut loose.

"Congratulations, you have been chosen as a winner in our competi--" beep, and the line was dead. Whoops, had I accidentally pressed the red button? I laughed. Hopefully this would be enough. But no such luck. The phone rang again. I really wanted to give them a piece of my mind, but this time it was a different number. Hmm, I thought, those buggers probably had several lines to bait people. Fine. I answered again. At first, all was silent, until a male voice spoke up.

"Elara?" he said carefully. The hairs in the back of my neck stood up. Mike! He must have gotten a different number somehow, probably from one of his friends. "Elara, I know you're there. Please let us talk like two reasonable adults."

My patience was really put to the test. If I hung up now, he would show up at my door within minutes. "Mike, what do you want?" I asked him irritatedly. Embarrassing silence at the other end. A soft sniffle. Dear Goodness, was he crying?! Hopefully not. Another sniffle and he continued, his voice softer and thinner than before.

"Elara, please, let us talk one more time. We can go to a cafe if you don't want me to come to the house, or we'll meet in a park. Please! I mean, that can't have been it, right? Let us talk.
Dear heaven, was he drunk again? That happened way too often. Especially when his friends edged him on.
"Elara? Elara, please, say something!" Mike pleaded.

I just snorted. "Mike, listen. Is it possible you had a few drinks?" I said, being straightforward.

"Oh Elara, just a couple of beers. Okay, maybe one or two schnapps glasses as well. You know how it is. Thomas his kid won the first game today, you know, in the club." Of course I knew. This used to happen on a daily basis. There was always a reason to have a few. "Oh Elara, Elara, do you even know how beautiful your name sounds? I just... Do you remember the first time we met and you told me your name? It was like a dream... Elara..." Oh, now this should be fun. While   (14)

Mike cried his heart out, I scrolled through websites on the computer. It was no use interrupting him now. Two minutes later he would be back and blaming me. For now all I could do is hope he would get it together soon.

Something crackled in the phone line. Someone was trying to call me again. Probably those sales reps again. In the half hour conversation with Mike, someone tried contacting me three times. It couldn't be Ellis. She didn't call people, she only sent texts and whatsapp messages. How persistent were these people? And my email was similarly at daggers drawn. Three new messages again. I only read the subject.

"Congratulations. You were chosen…" well, wasn't that new. I deleted the messages without reading them. I really had to do something about the spam. The sniffles at the other end of the phone line were getting quieter. The conversation was drawing to a close. To top it all off, my mobile was vibrating now. What was going on today? Ellis was probably bored and sending me one of her cat pictures. Whatever. Open… Oh, she had had time to write something. Oh, oh, I had six messages from her. Atypical. "El?" Asked the first one. Then a smiley. The next one. "Elara? Are you not reading your messages?" Then, "HELLO?" in all caps. "Goodness gracious, Elara, put Mike down!" the fifth demanded. She knew exactly whenever Mike called. And the last one. "Booh, read   (15) your messages. Not the phone ones." But I deleted them all, I thought. Then I realised which ones she could mean. Social networks. All right, who or what was trying to communicate with me this urgently? To the log-in. Waiting! Loading… and there they were. The same as on my phone, three messages again. The first one once again began with "Congratulations. You were chosen…" Impossible! A hacker, in my computer. But my phone vibrated again. "READ!" Ellis' voice demanded. Fine, fine. The second message!

"Hello Ms Jackson,
Unfortunately, we were unable to reach you on the phone. Nonetheless, we would like to congratulate you on your win. Please confirm your consent with your email address.
Regards,
Your Ireland Team"

What the… Oh, I had completely forgotten about Mike. He was still on the phone. I tried to listen in and found out that he was in the middle of our engagement. That could take a while yet. So I read the third message, or at least tried, as my notification bar showed eleven new popups. Ten people had tagged me. Why? I tried to regain control. Until the realisation hit me like a thunderclap. It really was a message from Kyran himself. Sweet Goodness gracious, what had I done? Sure, years ago I sent him a friendship request, which he had   (16) at least accepted quite quickly. What followed were numerous likes and a few odd comments, but this, now, was unbelievable. A sniffle at the other end of the phone. Mike was blowing his nose. I had to get rid of him now. Quickly, I scanned Kyran's message. My heart was racing.

"Hello Elara, thank you for taking part in our competition. I wanted to congratulate you personally. You won a seven day trip to Ireland. I am looking forward to meeting you. Lots of love, Kyran."

Attached were the terms and conditions. They proved that I had indeed won a trip to Ireland, including a personal guided tour with Kyran, plus a pub concert and a holiday home in the countryside. On top of it a dinner with the band and a tour through Dublin. My jaw dropped. I could only whisper into the phone.

"I can't believe this. I think I'm going mad."

Immediately, Mike bellowed back. "But you agreed when we bought the house. I really don't know..." he began, but I had to cut him off.

"Mike... Mike, please, I can't right now. Listen, write me a text when you have the time. I'll get back to you then. Take care!" And just like that I simply hung up. Again and again I read (17) the message. It couldn't possibly be true. It had to be a fake with the worst yet to come. I had meant to make it my goal never to open spam mail, and especially not for competitions. Where was I supposed to have taken part, anyway? Before I made my way through the terms and conditions, I first scrolled back to my activity feed of the last two weeks. I didn't have to search long. Just yesterday I had joined a competition at the last minute. At least that's what it said there.

My memory of doing that was more than foggy. The time, however, told me that I really had joined - while I was sleeping. Damn, I must have knocked the keys while asleep at my computer. I really needed to stop doing that. Who knew, one day I might end up with a house or a luxury car. So now it was time to read the conditions. There had to be a catch. But even after several reads I couldn't spot one. Everything seemed perfect. Journey to Amsterdam by train, then a ferry over to Ireland to be received by Kyran himself. All inclusive. This had to be a dream. When Ellis dropped in after work, she was flabbergasted.

"Oh goodness, that's what I call fate. Totally. Absolutely incredible. You… you are going, aren't you?" Ellis squinted at me. She knew me. When it came down to making decisions, I chickened out. It wasn't really my thing. And now to Ireland on my own. I was already starting to feel queasy. (18)

A little hesitantly, I shrugged and focused on the message. Again and again. Ellis could see my head spin.

"Oh no, you don't," she warned me.

"What? I didn't say anything yet," I muttered. Of course my thoughts were racing. And the more they did, the more scared I felt. I was already half leaning back when Ellis snapped at me.

"Goodness gracious, no, you don't. You are not giving up this trip. That is your chance to finally get out of here. Ireland. Goodness, it can't possibly get better, and on top of it all you get your Kyran. What do you have to lose? I'm telling you now, if you cancel this trip we're over and I swear to you I will sic Mike on you every single day," she threatened. She was serious. Sure, she was right. What did I have to lose. I could always write my column during the journey and I had some holiday left at the supermarket anyway, which wasn't busy right now. I just had to confirm the mail.

My fingers shook as they moved over the keyboard. Ellis looked over my shoulder and saw me hesitate. In a moment of inattention her fingers flew over my keys and the mail sent.

"Done!" I stared up in the grinning face of my friend.

"Say, can anyone else come along on that trip?" she asked a few minutes later. Sadly, this wasn't the case. (19)

Secretly, I wished for her company, then I wouldn't be so alone. Nonetheless, I was excited. I felt like a teenager.

Chapter Two

The time until my journey stretched for two endless months. Finally the day came. My bag was packed with necessary and unnecessary bits and bobs. Ellis took me all the way to Amsterdam, as she wanted to reward her holiday with a grand shopping tour if Ireland was out of the question. Of course Mike had caught wind of the trip and had been making digs at me the entire time. Things like "Are you trying to catch up on your lost youth now?", or "Do you really need some young shag buddy now? He doesn't want you anyway. It's all just a scam," all of which hit me hard below the belt. On the other hand, it reinforced my decision to go.

Two hours later we finally arrived. The boat was already in the harbour and people were rushing back and forth. Now it was time to say goodbye. Ellis hugged me close and joked around.

"Hey, I could hide in the suitcase. I'm small enough. Oh, and don't you dare text less than three times a day! And you better take ten thousand pictures of you and Kyran. Come here, sweetie!" she demanded and pulled me close again. Tears welled up in her eyes. "Oh, just go and get yourself a hot guy."

I hugged her one more time before she took off in her little red corsa. Here I was, with my suitcase and bag. On the one hand I felt like running away, on the other I felt the thrill of adventure. The ship's bell rang. It was time to go aboard. I pulled out my boarding pass and was given directions to a small cabin, which I had to share with another woman, else I would have had to pay extra. For now, I was alone. That meant I could choose my bed. They were bunk beds, nothing special, but enough for my needs. The ship had a breakfast buffet, and I wanted to eat a bite. Before the trip I had taken a pill against the nausea. It was working well, which was why I felt a small pang of hunger.

No sooner had I reached the buffet than I was rudely pushed aside. A younger woman with, well, let's say heavy bones was approaching. She was huffing and kept having to cough because of the exertion. However, this was over as soon as she had reached the food. I didn't even pay attention to her. My bread roll looked quite poor against her plate, but it was enough for me.

The ship horn sounded again and we soon left the harbour. Just like on the Titanic, I ran to the railing and leaned over it. I followed all the people that had grouped together there and waved at their loved ones. I didn't care. But wait, wasn't that a familiar face? Strike a light, it really was Mike waving at (22) me. How could he? On the one hand it was soothing to see a familiar face, but internally I was boiling with anger at his intentions. Thank God he wasn't on board. I quickly looked in a different direction.

The saltwater filled my nose and put a film on my lips, while the wind mussed through my hair. It was still quite cool here. For the time being I went back below deck, especially since it started to rain lightly. In one room I found several empty seats, surrounded by books and with a sea view. I grabbed a book on Ireland and paged through it while my eyes scanned the water surface. My eyelids grew heavier and heavier. Shortly before falling asleep, I decided to make my way back to my cabin to freshen up and potentially have a nap.

Even from quite a distance I could hear the permanent laughter of that woman from the buffet. She laughed and snorted and seemed to want to draw attention to herself. Not enough that she was dressed quite unflatteringly, no, she made sure everything went exactly her way. Everyone who stood in her path was flattened, and everyone who tried to flee was loudly called back.

"Where can I play some parlour games? Where can I watch TV? Where can I take a phone call without being disturbed? When do we arrive?" And, and, and. Add to that her   (23) shrill voice interspersed with the continuous coughing. I quickly fled into my cabin. It was still empty. At least I could freshen up. Ten minutes later I already felt better. The soft rocking motion lulled me somewhat and I lay down. I quickly started dozing, until a voice made me start up. The woman from the buffet was running down the hall in front of the door, yelling into her phone. I had to press my pillow on my ears. Which didn't help much. Suddenly the door was slammed open and the woman stood in the middle of the room. I was flabbergasted, what was this person thinking? Seconds away from my outburst, she stretched her fat hand in my direction.

"Rachel. Rachel Kuhn," she said abruptly, her phone still on her ear, only to continue yelling at it. "No, mother, I am not in the cafeteria. Yes, I had something to eat. No, there are no celebrities here. Yes, mother, I am in my cabin now," and the door to the washroom fell shut, emitting the sounds of her struggle. The cabins were not very large. Wait a second, did she say her cabin? My gaze fell on the large suitcase on the other bed. The name tag made me fear the worst. Rachel Kuhn, it said in colourful letters. Fabulous, so that was my roommate. This was going to be fun.

Full of fear I glanced up, realising that I was laying in a bunk bed. I had to swallow at the thought. Loud, but hardly ladylike sounds were coming from the bathroom. This was   (24) getting better by the second. I was about to lay down on my side, when the door was slammed open and Rachel exited. Even though she had freshened up, I could see and smell her odours. Skeptically, she eyed first me and then the bed. I soon realised what her look was supposed to tell me.

Oh, I... I didn't mean to be pushy. If you would prefer the bottom bunk, it's not a problem for me." I sounded almost whiny. The mere idea of sleeping in the top bunk made me uncomfortable. If I needed to go to the toilet, I would have to climb down every time, and every movement went through the entire bed. On the other hand, if Rachel were to climb down... No, the thought could not be finished.

"No worries at all, but if you insist... Erm..." She gave me an inquiring look, until I got what she wanted.

"Oh. Elara. My name is Elara Jackson." I was about to offer my hand, but my bedding flew in my face, and before I knew it she had climbed past me into my bed. Ok, so I moved to the top one. I didn't much care anymore and I gave in to my fate. No sooner had I put my head down that I heard Rachel snore. It wasn't, how should I say, soft and thoughtful, no, more like penetrating and very loud, not to mention some sounds that were not coming from her mouth. My headphones were giving it their all, while I turned to face the wall and tried to   (25) sleep. Regarding the time, it seemed to pass in a blink. As soon as I had closed my eyes, Rachel woke me again.

"Ooh, isn't this exciting. Only five hours and we are in Ireland. Isn't it exciting? Man, I have so much left to do." She swung her legs down and the door to the bathroom slammed shut. A full half hour she stayed inside, before squeezing out and grabbing her bag.

"Not hungry? I sure am, sea journeys always make me hungry, and if you're not quick the others will eat everything." The door slammed shut again. This place is like a bad movie, I thought. But she was right. It was time to get up. I meant to freshen up again, but the bathroom was beyond ridiculous. A strong smell assaulted me and towels were strewn across the floor. Don't fuss, I thought. It will be over by this afternoon. Time to soldier on.

I tried to clean up the chaos as best I could, after all I didn't want anyone to think I was a disaster. I spent the rest of the day as much as possible inside souvenir - and bookshops. As we got closer to the harbour, dozens of announcements in different languages came out of the speakers. Not long now. My excitement grew. I quickly applied the few makeup products I had brought along and put on elegant, but not stuck-up clothes. After all, it wasn't every day that I met a (26) star. I looked at myself in the mirror. I still looked quite young for my age. Almost no wrinkles, hazelnut-brown eyes, middle-length, ash blonde hair, and my figure was still great, too. Maybe no longer that of a firm twenty year-old, but neither that of an old sixty year-old.

Thank God I was done when Rachel blew in. I quickly grabbed my suitcase and made a break for it. The hallway was already packed. Suitcase after suitcase was pushed down the hallway. Chattering people of all sizes and ages. And in the middle of it all was, of course, Rachel, pushing her way through like a fighter behemoth. The masses accumulated on deck and everyone wanted to be the first to set foot on the green island. I didn't care. After all, I had someone to pick me up, or so I hoped. Now I was feeling nauseous with excitement. I didn't even know what to talk about with Kyran. Maybe he wouldn't even like me. Would he even be able to understand me, and was my English good enough? What, if he only spoke Irish? Oh, come on, Elara, it's going to be fine, I tried to calm myself. English was really no problem for me, after all I had followed my passion for the English language and taken several classes. After all, you never knew.

Chapter Three

As soon as I entered the deck, the wind whipped around my ears. Combined with the salt of the ocean, the green grass, and the ship's diesel, paired with the odours of several people, which reminded me of Rachel again. Goodness gracious, how would I recognise Kyran? Maybe he wouldn't even look like his profile. And if he wasn't here? Where should I go then? I kept an iron grip on the piece of paper with the terms and conditions and climbed down the ramp. The people dispersed quickly. Some boarded busses, others were picked up by taxis, and others again walked on foot or drove off by car. The crowd quickly became lighter. If Kyran should be here, how would I know where? And if so, wouldn't he draw a crowd, simply since he was famous? I felt hot now, even though the wind was cool on my forehead. Not much of Ireland's beauty was visible for now, but the call of wild freedom beckoned more and more strongly. I took my small bottle of coke, took a sip, and sat down on my suitcase. There it was again. A permanent cough. Should I look around? That wasn't necessary. Rachel stormed right past me. She wheezed and coughed with every step. Her blouse was already showing visible sweat stains and I prayed that she would pass me by. I couldn't have been more wrong. An old Ford

Mustang Oldtimer appeared from out of nowhere and a guy with leather jacket and sunglasses got out, followed by two men a la body builder. As soon as he had looked in my direction, a scream ripped through Rachel and she flailed her hands and feet to get to him. Goodness gracious, was this her brother or…

"Kyran!" she screeched again and again, "Kyran!" Then she robbed on and I could already see her run him over. If only for the two muscled men. They tried to stop her as much as possible. Which they didn't manage without difficulty. Only now that the small shock had passed, Kyran glimpsed me and the paper in my hand. He quickly fixed his glasses and hat and stomped over to me.

"Elara Jackson?" he asked and I could only nod. He held out his hand and I took it quickly, shaking. "Welcome. So you two are my winners. Welcome once again to Ireland. These two gentlemen will now accompany you to the accommodation. Everything else we can discuss this afternoon. Enjoy your day." He tapped his hat and climbed back into the car. The two men sat one in the front and one in the back. Kyran drove the car, but didn't seem one bit interested in talking to us, which went completely past Rachel. She talked non-stop. That was just what I needed. To share my stay with this person of all people. Here, then, was the infamous catch. But there   (29) was no helping it. I tried to enjoy the landscape as much as possible. We went from the harbour straight to the motorway. At high speed we passed green hills and small lakes, past old ruins and windswept trees. It was truly astounding to see all this. Between the sometimes quite modern, newly built houses, I kept catching glimpses of old, decaying buildings or otherwise old houses that had not been fixed up in years or whose owner was missing the necessary change. So this was the famous and mysterious Ireland. Ah well, I hoped that once we had arrived the beautiful nature would open itself up to me at least. Was I imagining it or was this Kyran always speeding up? No, it really was the case. No word passed his lips. He just grunted to himself. His sunglasses hung so low on his face that he was unrecognisable, as well as his large hat. I didn't know if that was his thing, but I considered that kind of behaviour impolite. Rachel wasn't bothered by it in the slightest. She chatted and chatted and didn't realise that nobody replied to her. From time to time Kyran stole a glance at the back, or maybe I simply imagined it. What felt like a hundred miles later we exited the motorway into a side street, or rather a dirt track. It had no real road surface, only a kind of path on both sides and a line of green growing down its middle. Every pothole made the car bounce and I felt it mightily in my lower extremities, which was starting to cause me to pray that we would get there soon. Because I   (30) had a need that I was not going to explain here and in front of these people. So I tried to take my mind off the situation. What kind of person was this Kyran, anyway? I mean, fine, he made great music, was successful and looked quite good as well. Hmm, something about him gave me pause. Wasn't he taller in the pictures, his hair fuller? He actually seemed a bit older here. Well, I knew that photos could be edited, but this wasn't fair, I thought. The car was slowing down, and after numerous meadows and tree-lined avenues we came to a stop in front of a small property. A white house, enclosed by an old, almost rotted wooden fence, was peeking out right by the side of the path. A semicircular, brown door, kept simple, appeared to be the entrance. The little house had small, rectangular windows, and when I looked around the building I found a large garden with two trees. From afar I could hear a brook burble along. But no neighbours far and wide. Only in the far distance could I see the outline of a farm. Next to the house were umpteen meadows and lawns. So here was supposed to be our domicile. Well, here was to hoping we would at least have separate rooms. Otherwise I would sleep on the sofa.

In the meantime, Kyran stayed put and said, glancing into the rearview mirror, "This, my ladies, is your territory for the next days. The fridge is full, so is the pantry. There's a fireplace and everything else you'll see once you're inside.   (31)

Have a great stay. Sean here will pick you ladies up around evening and take you to Ky... erm, to my concert." With these words Sean got out and held the door open for us. Rachel stomped ahead like a steamroller. Sean still struggled with her suitcase, while I took my smaller one myself. I meant to ask this Kyran how the key situation would be handled, but he was deeply engrossed in a phone conversation. I held my suitcase in my hand and spotted a key stuck in the lock. Oh, ok, in that case I was relieved. I took a few steps before I realised that I had left my handbag in the car. That would be the icing on the cake, to run through Ireland without money or phone. I left the suitcase for a moment, which was immediately snatched up by Sean and carried to the house. I ran back to the car. In the meantime Kyran had stepped out, I assumed for better signal or to have a smoke. Although I had read in his profile that he didn't smoke. Nevermind. My bag was thank God still on the back seat. I had to climb in to grab it. Suddenly I heard Kyran, who was waving his arms, angry and annoyed. I could just hear a few snippets of dialogue, and I think I didn't like it at all.

"Yeah, sure, I dropped the chicks off at the house. But no, not a problem, you know me. Yeah, sure. The program continues. Sure! Before they know it the concert is over and we can bugger off again. Just leave it to me, I'll pull it off, you'll see, they won't notice anything. Little bit of sight seeing,   (32) a few souvenirs and they're on cloud nine." He only spotted me then, coming out of the woodwork. Should I address the issue or ignore it and pretend I hadn't heard anything?

"Oh, yes, there's the silly thing. Completely forgot it," I said shakily and demonstratively lifted my bag in the air. Kyran sucked on his cigarette and tried to give me a small smile, which in my opinion looked more like a deceitful one. The blaze smouldered, like the top of a volcano just before it erupted. The phone still in his hand, he quickly turned away and murmured into the phone.

"I... Erm, I'll speak to you later. I think we're on thin ice here." He quickly got in the car and called for that Sean. Then he once again tapped his hat as a quick goodbye. The tires squealed and he was gone. This had to be a nightmare, I thought. Internally I only hoped the days would pass soon and I cursed myself for partaking in the competition and for listening to Ellis when she told me to go. Now I was standing here with Rachel and, if I wasn't completely mistaken, a ruined trip. What was it my grandma used to say, if there's nothing good in a day, try to make the best of it. Alright, I had no other choice. Driving or flying back was too expensive anyway, since it was all combined. Time to grit my teeth. Maybe it wouldn't be all that bad.

First I looked at my phone. Of course, a million messages from Mike, and three from Ellis. At least I had signal here and immediately shot a couple of pictures, which I sent to my friend. I wanted to call her later as well. Regarding Mike, I should really have done myself the favour not to open the messages, but I am a woman and naturally curious. It ranged from "Hey, arrived safe and sound?" to "Hope the weather is nice" or "You could have told me you were going", to several with emojis and the last one, "I miss you so. Come home safe. We have to talk. Please." With that came a kissing emoji. Urgh, I could feel bile rising in my throat. Goodness gracious, I only now realised that I was still standing outside. I could already hear Rachel bang about inside. She was just spreading out in the kitchen. From the outside the house looked quite small, but once inside, I found it to be really cute. A small hallway began at the entrance and led straight into the eat-in kitchen. On the right side of the wall, a small kitchen was built into a niche, with a counter to sit at in front of it. Right behind it, a two-person sofa with flowery covers stood in the middle of the room. In front of that a wooden chest to be used as a table, as well as a wing chair in striped reds. To finish it off, an armoire and a TV table with a flat screen TV. In the corner, a fireplace was happily smouldering. They still heated with turf here, and it gave off a pleasant smell. At the end of the house were two small rooms with a bed, a   (34) chest of drawers, and a closet each. The bathroom at the start of the hallway was equipped with a shower, sink, and toilet. A small hatch presumably served as ventilation. Rachel went through the contents of the fridge and was rewarded with some sausages and toast. Now that I thought about it, we had yet to exchange a word. I usually wasn't the convivial type, but it seemed that it would be unavoidable here.

"Hello," I grinned and courageously approached her. "We haven't introduced ourselves yet. I am Elara Jackson," and I held out my hand. Rachel quickly wiped her mouth and chewed on her toast.

"Yeah... hrmph... I know. I am Rachel Kuhn. We already introduced ourselves on the boat. You took part in the competition, too, isn't that wild. I mean, here in Ireland with Godfather Kyran. Increeeeedible." While she was eating, bits of food kept falling out of her mouth and I only laughed dispiritedly. This would be an experience. Weren't there plans for a dinner with Kyran? Oh dear. So now we had gotten to know each other a little, and we quickly arranged who would sleep in which room. I also finally got the chance to change. It would still be two hours until we were picked up. Where we would go then, I didn't know. So I decided to wear something casual. Ripped jeans, black blouse, and ankle boots. It didn't take me long to wash my hair, and I wandered outside. (35)

Dusk seemed to be heralding itself very slowly. The wind freshened up a little and made my ash-blonde, middle-length locks dance in the air. I breathed in and out deeply. Actually, what had I imagined the air to be like here? Hmm, let's see, maybe fresher or cleaner? From the door I took a few steps around the house, to where the garden was seamlessly integrated. From outside I could hear Rachel munching away, and how she was zapping aimlessly through the TV channels. She searched fruitlessly for a German channel.

"Oh, look, they barely have any TV channels. Uh, I found MTV, maybe Kyran is there, too," she told me. Even though it was utter nonsense to see said singer on TV. Although he had had a hit or two in the past. Ah well, at least Rachel was kept busy. Step by step I slowly made my way away from the house and down the property. The further I got into the open, the fresher the air seemed to me. A bit on one side I could hear a small brook burble. My curiosity was piqued. The premise ended almost imperceptibly at the brook and bordered onto a kind of grove. It wasn't as afforested as a proper grove. Only a few trees were growing close together, but also allowed an immediate look further across the neighbouring meadows and fields. As far as the eye could see, I spotted occasional hills, bordered with fences, and wild flowers and bushes were having a tryst. The wind   (36) whistled through the trees and seemed to get trapped in their crowns. Someone had gotten creative and transformed a tree trunk into a bench. I still had another hour until the wannabe-Kyran would come to pick us up. Before I went inside and listened to Rachel's music program, I rather stayed outside and enjoyed the silence. Surprisingly, the log was not cold at all and actually cosy as well. My eyes looked out over the fields once again. Slowly, I closed them and listened to the wind and the soft, but steady burble. My lungs filled with oxygen. Only now did it sink in just where I was. Kyran and Rachel were all but forgotten, they could stay where they were. I enjoyed the here and now and had to admit, I had been wrong. Here, now, with the air in my lungs, I could feel it. The nature, the meadow smelling of fresh, rain-soaked grass, the forests smelling of resin and fallen leaves, the brook itself made me smell the crystal clear water. And mingling with it all I breathed the herby, salty air, and it smelled like freedom.

Indescribable and fantastic. Even the wind smelled like salt and freedom. I could not say just how long I sat there. I had completely lost track of time, and I was sitting utterly relaxed on this log, as if I was rooted to it. I didn't even register the voices that were dully trying to get through to me. Only a soft shake brought me back to the present. Sean, our driver, had been waiting for me for ten minutes. Embarrassing   (37) that I hadn't realised. He thought I had fallen asleep. I allowed him to direct me to the car only with reluctance and slouched into the backseat. No Kyran! At least that was something. Rachel was ever dependable.

"Where is Kyran, though? Are we driving to him now? What is happening then? Oh, isn't this exciting? Us and Kyran, who else should be this lucky? Fabulous!" Yeah, we were lucky, I thought. Lucky that it wasn't raining. I grinned to myself. Sean just about saw it in the rearview mirror and could not stop the tiniest grin, especially since I rolled my eyes a little before looking out of the window again. Rachel chatted on as usual. About how this had never happened to her before and what else would be waiting for us. My ears switched off, that is until her fat fingers started poking my arm.

"What?" I asked, completely bewildered. Rachel rolled her eyes.
"Do you have jet lag or something? I asked if you kipped in the garden? I mean, everything is crawling with vermin out there. I'm quite happy that we're finally going into town now. Ooh, I wonder if he'll give us a private concert? What do you think?" she asked Sean. He just shrugged with one shoulder and tried to smile. I muttered softly under my breath and gave Rachel her reply, even though I knew she was not listening anymore. (38)

"I was just enjoying the fresh air. The freedom... The, oh, nevermind." I sighed softly, not noticing that Sean had understood me full well. We drove back onto the motorway in the direction of the city. As soon as we got there, things went back to their earlier rapid pace. Sean directed us to a restaurant, which turned out to be half pub, half fish 'n' chips-shop. It smelled of fat, fish, and a little sweat. Everyone talked over each other. People came and went and there was barely any room, but Sean pushed us through the throng and to a corner table near a door that kept opening and closing. Rachel clapped her hands, unable to contain her excitement at the possibility of finally getting something to eat or whatever. A waiter got us a menu and immediately Rachel stuck her nose in it so far that I feared she would eat that as well. What was all this about, I wondered. It all seemed like a bad dream. Either someone was completely taking the piss or they were trying to polish us off as quickly and cheaply as possible. Where was that Sean? I searched for him in the crowd and spotted him, of course, with his phone near the bar. He nodded a lot and kept glancing in our direction. As soon as I looked back, he lowered his head in shame and made sure to end the call quickly.

After a glass of Shandy, or perhaps just beer, he made his way back to us. He met our eyes for a mere second   (39) before he said dejectedly, "Erm, Kyran apologises profusely, but something else has come up tonight. He is asking you to eat a bite and he will see you at nine pm in the pub next door."

That was the icing on the cake. Rachel's mouth immediately twisted downwards and I thought she was just about to slap Sean, but instead she took the menu and ordered up a storm. Well, our table soon reflected that. The whole mess got on my nerves and my appetite, so I merely ate a few chips with vinegar and some chicken. They actually weren't bad for this hole-in-the-wall. I had assumed we would see and experience some more of the city. Maybe that was the plan for the next day, at least I hoped so. I could happily eat and listen to music at home, and yes, there I had no Kyran, but then again it wasn't like he was here, either. Apart from that early greeting, regarding which my inner sense told me right away that that had not been Kyran. It would be interesting to see where else this trickery would go.

After dinner Sean accompanied us to the pub next door. He had at least reserved two seats. These were not right by the stage, but in the third row, and the view was still good. We were served Guinness, but Rachel didn't like it. She said it was too strong for her, so she ordered a glass of wine. In the meantime, Sean placed himself by the bar and also had a large pint of beer. Here was hoping he knew what   (40) he was doing. More and more people were arriving at rapid pace and it was getting very crowded, even at the table. In the jostle and throng, one elbow after the other hit me in the back. Great, if this went on all night I would have a thousand bruises by morning and the trip would be *so* over for me. The light was dimmed now and a chair placed on the stage, and finally Kyran arrived. He was wearing black jeans and a jeans shirt with the top buttons undone, along with brown boots and of course his hat, but miraculously no sunglasses. Yes, this was clearly Kyran. But why had he gotten some joke to stand in for him at the beginning? Rachel was completely over the moon and it was clear to see. Sweat was running down her face, which was glowing red. Again and again she clapped her hands and yelled "Kyran, Kyran". Goodness gracious, this was embarrassing, especially since some people were amusedly turning around to look at us. Kyran, too, was just glancing at us, and I felt ready for the earth to swallow me whole. Then he tuned his guitar, and... it rang. Everyone was looking around. Me too, until I realised that they were looking at me, and Kyran was staring in annoyance, too.

"Would it be possible for the young lady to answer her phone so we can begin," he said dryly and everyone laughed. Only Rachel glared at me venomously and hissed.

"Do you have to draw so much attention to yourself? How embarrassing you are, really!" she growled and turned demonstratively away from me to make cow eyes at Kyran. I quickly pulled out my phone and glanced at it. Great, who else, Mike. I quickly muted him and tried to listen to the music. I had to admit that when he started, I was immediately smitten. His voice was truly unique and so was the way he played the guitar as if it was bedded on clouds. He played old classics, such as: Whiskey in the Jar, or Dirty Old Town, but also a lot of new and covered songs. I no longer noticed the pub bursting at the seams, too transfixed was I by his music. He played for more than two hours. The thunderous standing ovation was certain. So were his fans, who surged forward as one to get an autograph, including Rachel, who was fighting her way through the crowd.

I had been planning to get an autograph myself, but I decided against it in the face of this crowd. Sean had stolen himself outside instead, and I followed his lead. He was standing outside the door for a smoke, like some other people. Should I try to start a conversation with him? Oh, whatever, after all I did want to know what would happen next.

"Hey! So what's going on next?" I asked him directly.

He coughed, since he clearly hadn't expected me. He looked around as if he was searching for someone else. "I, erm, I am not sure yet. I will be informed soon. Erm... Maybe you should wait inside. Your friend is probably lonely and looking for you," he stuttered. Apparently I had hit the nail on the head here. Another little puppy waiting for its master's commands. Great! So I tried to get back into the pub while other people tried to get out. Someone bumped into me hard enough that I stumbled and fell against a flower pot. Thank goodness for that, too, because otherwise I would have been impaled on the fence behind it. Dead on the fence in Ireland, a great headline. My trousers were covered in soil and I was just brushing myself down when a large group of people surged outside, led by Kyran. After a few words with them the crowd dispersed into nothing.

"Hey, Kyran, great concert. We have to repeat that some time," a man called out and carried a drum inside.

An older lady came running up. "Oh, Kyran, can I please have an autograph for my daughter?" Kyran nodded, scribbled something on her picture, and turned to Sean. Almost out of reach, but close enough for me to hear, the singer started to vent.

(43)

"Wow, what a Gig. The place was crammed again. Okay, what's up with the chicks? If you could fend them off for another couple hours I would be grateful. I really need some fresh air, a bath, and a beer. Believe me, these German shrews get on my nerves like nothing else. That screeching and drooling. Disgusting. I…" He didn't get any further, since Sean kept nodding in my direction. Kyran now finally realised what was going on. But he still made no move to apologise. For my part, I continued innocently brushing down my trousers as if I hadn't heard anything. Such an arse, I thought to myself, but I smiled. My hand gave a short wave and I indicated that I was going back inside. But in my thoughts I flipped them off, and I prepared myself to leave this place as quickly as possible. Enough with the lies. Should I bother Rachel with this? Hmm, it was worth a try. So into the pub I went and I didn't have to search long. She was still by the stage, chatting to the drummer.

"Rachel, say, doesn't this all seem outrageous to you?" I asked, not paying attention to the guy.

Her eyes shone when she turned to me. "Yes, isn't it? Completely amazing. And I was beginning to think I would never get lucky. But this, here, is sheer madness. Look here, I got an autograph from Kyran!" (44)

She was so over the moon that I didn't have the heart to ruin it for her. Just before I left I tapped her arm again.

"Hey, Rachel, what's the name of the hicktown we are staying at again?" I had completely forgotten the name, while Rachel studied everything that had to do with Kyran.

"Oh, erm... ah yes, Kilmessan it was. Right."

I thanked her and told her in leaving, "If this Kyran or Sean show up, can you please tell them that I went ahead. This is all a bit too much for me." She nodded imperceptibly and I made myself scarce. My head was starting to throb as well. Probably from the air inside the pub. Now I was standing in front of the pub, not sure where to go. Should I dare to walk around the city on my own or drive back to Kilmessan? Well, I really didn't feel like celebrating anymore. A taxi rink caught my eye, and when I asked the driver how much it would be to get to Kilmessan, he stared at me in disbelief. Or maybe it was pity. In any case he grinned and gave me a price. Yes, it was ridiculously high, but I would rather go back than celebrate with Kyran or whatever else. When we drove down the highway, it was pitch black. Only the occasional street lamp lit the dark, while all along the roadside the small lights of houses flashed by here and there. I was getting a bit chilly and pulled my cardigan tighter around my shoulders. In Kilmessan I had to explain the way to the driver, which   (45) wasn't easy in the darkness. I only remembered the way a moment before. So I indicated for him to go down the small alley. I hoped he would not misunderstand me or would turn out to be a rapist after all. A few metres further I spotted the house. Unharmed, I got out and was glad that the key was still in the lock. So this really was paradise on earth. Especially here in the countryside. On the other hand, nobody would hear you scream if you were lying dead in the bushes. I shivered a little, quickly paid the driver and went inside for the time being. Oh, no Rachel babbling away. But her chaos was omnipresent. I quickly cleaned away the worst of it. I couldn't help myself, I was too used to it from home. I checked if Rachel had at least left me anything to eat. A sausage and a slice of toast were quickly spotted. That was enough for me. I even found a bottle of wine. It was dry, but didn't taste as awful as I feared. In the little pantry I found a few torches and candles. The night was so beautiful that I decided to go back to the old tree trunk and hide away there for a while. Behind the house I even spotted an old bowl with wood in it and decided to make a small campfire. Everything was there, a fire bowl, wood and turf anyway, all that was missing were the marshmallows, but whatever, I couldn't have everything. The torches lit the way to the tree trunk. The fire burned quickly when I lit it, and in the background the brook burbled along like a soporific melody. Yes, this was the place for me.   (46)

Now the wine tasted almost like good whiskey. I leaned back with a sigh. Even though I was a little afraid of creepy crawlies, I didn't much care when I was here. Now, at night, when the frost covered the grass and the trees, the scents of nature were intensified. I absorbed everything like a sponge and grinned happily to myself. The dewy mist even covered my cheeks and pearled down my face, until I realised that I was actually crying. Why? I was doing great after all. Maybe it was all a bit too much after all and I was losing it? No, no, I thought. Everything was fine. So I leaned back once again and let it all out. I didn't care what I was doing; after all, nobody could see me. The bottle of wine was already half empty, and I didn't even notice the lights appear in front of the house. Two doors slammed and every light in the house was turned on. The TV was turned up to full volume, of course showing MTV. Rachel had to be back. I didn't care, I stayed where I was. Steps came closer. Nothing against the young woman, but I had no intention of talking to her, especially not about how great the evening with Kyran had been. Booh, Kyran. Oh. Oh, Kyran. It couldn't be. The guy was really standing here in the garden, and he... he seemed really angry.

"What were you thinking? You can't just bugger off without saying anything like that! All the things that could   (47) have happened. You are my responsibility. Didn't you consider that at all? How irresponsible that was of you. You could have told someone." Well, that was quite something else. To appear here in front of me and play the big man. Incredible. My tears weren't quite dry when I quickly wiped them away. But not quickly enough that he didn't see.

"Wait, were you crying? I... I am sorry, I didn't know that you..."

The last thing I needed was pity from that guy. All the beauty of nature aside, I was boiling. "How dare you? First you send this wannabe replacement and think nobody will notice, and then you let people conceal you for some reason, and then you make stupid jokes about the typical German skirts, who are oh so dumb. Who is laughable now? Everything here was some kind of joke. I should have cancelled the trip. Nothing against you, your music is really great, but this whole thing is such a joke. And also, I am not homesick, if that is why you think I am crying. Yes, I cried, but only because nature overwhelmed me. I know someone like you can never understand that. You are probably thinking oh, stupid city chick, cries because of some grass and fields, but whatever, I don't care what you think. It is like it is, how could someone like you understand that." I was loaded, the safety was off, and I was shooting blind. Had I maybe fired too   (48) much? Somewhat self-consciously I gnawed on my lower lip and crossed my arms. Kyran was staring, completely aghast. He seemed to be looking for words. Instead of an answer he got Sean, who snuck closer and whispered something. The singer merely nodded and muttered something like, "Get yourself a coffee, I'll be there soon," and the driver jogged away and Kyran was standing in front of me, his own arms crossed. I on the other hand had started to shake at my own courage, and to control the shaking I sat back down on the tree trunk. Kyran was standing around as if he wasn't sure what to do with himself, until he finally grabbed a piece of wood and tossed it into the fire. It smouldered immediately and the flames licked it hungrily. When the young man started speaking, I flinched a bit.

"I... I am sorry. I didn't mean to put the blame on you, but when you just up and left I finally realised that I had messed up. You see, what I said in front of the pub, I didn't really mean it. It's just that when we started this raffle, it was my manager's idea. It went well for a few years, but then it got worse. The girls got more and more bizarre. It even happened once that one was lying naked on my bed and stalked me wherever I went. It got too much for me, but my manager insisted. He said we would do it just one more year and then stop. I just snapped. Can you forgive me?"   (49)

He looked me in the eyes and held out his hand. First I hesitated, but then I gripped it and nodded silently. Forgiving someone looked different, I knew. Silence fell for a moment.

"And what was going on with this replacement?" I dug deeper. Kyran rolled his eyes.

"Oh, him. Yes, I know that was a stupid plan. To be perfectly honest, I didn't feel like sightseeing and asked my pal Pete to stand in for me. Well, I have to admit that he's done that before once in awhile. I do feel ashamed about that. But I thought, whatever, it was just that one more time anyway." Well, those were some great future prospects, I thought. I couldn't bring myself to care much either way. Who knew what I could still believe from this guy. So I got up, grabbed a torch, and was about to go back to the house.

"Goodnight!" I said to him, meaning to simply leave him behind, but Kyran held me back for a moment.

"Say, about the crying, that was a joke, right? You're playing around with me as revenge." He winked at me, but I shook my head.

"No. I know this goes completely over your head, but it really was the beauty of nature. It was... Nevermind." Again I walked towards the house. Before I had reached the door, I could hear steps behind me. Kyran was following me quickly.

"I had no idea. I mean, of course I am stunned to hear that, but to be honest, I get it. Listen, what if I said I wanted to properly apologise. What would you say to a small excursion tomorrow morning? I'll pick you up at eight. Alright?" he asked, and before I could reply he snapped his fingers as if to say, all done. I didn't care anyway and I just shrugged. In my head I was already at the next airport, which I was going to go to tomorrow morning. Kyran sounded his car's horn and Sean zipped out of the house, his face flushed red, while I found a highly amused Rachel inside.

"Well, you gave us a good scare. To just scarper like that," she purred. I gave up. To argue with her now was pointless. I had told her that I was going back to the house. Either way she was now sitting on the sofa with her bag of crisps and watched her shows. I couldn't stand it anymore. The wine and the good air did their best and I fell tiredly into bed. I no longer heard any of Rachel's music and certainly not the permanent buzzing of my phone. Ellis and Mike were completely forgotten. Goodness gracious, she was going to rip me a new one if I didn't text or at least send pictures soon. At least I could blame the signal being so bad here, even though that would be a lie, but should I confess just how catastrophic everything here was? No, she would only take it to heart and curse herself for making me go. Oh yes, and regarding Mike, he could rot for all I cared. Even though I wouldn't put it   (51) past him to jump on the next plane to get here. Anything but that, I thought with a sudden sense of dread. I quickly typed a message to Ellis to tell her that everything was fine and I would totally get back to her tomorrow. After I received a short "OK" I sank into the pillows.

Chapter Four

To my surprise I was up again very early in the morning. Six a.m. was not usually my time, but as I had turned in early yesterday I woke up accordingly. I felt surprisingly good. Rachel was still snoring, thank goodness. Of course she had forgotten to turn off the TV again, and her crisps were scattered everywhere. So I went to the bathroom, had a wash, and got dressed. Today I decided on tight blue jeans with a white blouse and black boots. I quickly cleaned up my flatmate's residue and wiped down some of the tables and closets, while also brewing some coffee and eating toast with marmalade. The sun was very carefully peeking out through the clouds. For now it wasn't strong enough to fight its way through, but that did not deter me from grabbing my coffee and going outside. It was a little chilly, so I put on my leather jacket and made my way to the small stream. This morning it seemed to be even clearer. I knelt down and held my hands in the water. It was so wonderfully cool and crystal clear that it took my breath away. Coffee in hand, I knelt like that for a while and listened to the soft sounds of the brook. Here I felt closer to nature than anywhere else. Light frost was still covering the grass, the plants and trees, and every beam of light seemed to bring them all to life all over again.   (53)

I could see exactly how they were imbued with new life. I sighed to myself and before I knew it, I heard someone clear their throat behind me. I didn't want to wake up from this dream, but turned around and blinked against the sunlight until I realised who was standing in front of me. Kyran! Goodness gracious, I had completely forgotten about him.

"Oh. It's you. I… completely forgot about you. Sorry," I said and quickly got up. He was grinning again.

"I had expected you to still be curled up in bed. When I knocked, nothing stirred, and I didn't want to be rude and just burst in. I am ten minutes early after all. Well, until I saw the footsteps in the grass," he said chipperly.

Of course I immediately spoiling for a fight again. "What is that supposed to mean? Expected me to still be in bed? You think that just because we are city folks, we are in the habit of staying in bed till all hours? You underestimate us, or at least me," I hissed at him, though I felt immediately sorry for it. He was still grinning and raised his hands in defense.

"I didn't mean to insult you. It is just that most people who come here into nature are really knackered during the adjustment period. I apologise." He held out his hand and I briskly reached out for it, until he pointed at the gate and my coffee and I understood. (54)

"Oh. Oh yeah, I am just going to take my mug inside and nip to the bathroom, then we can go." Before I left I turned around one more time and asked him, "Erm, what am I supposed to tell Rachel? I think she will surely wonder or worry where I am." But as always Kyran just laughed and told me it would all be fine. Her day was already planned, and he pointed at Sean's number in his phone. Sean had agreed to do a city tour with Rachel and, what do you know, she hadn't had any complaints. As if she would worry about me. Either way I quickly went to the bathroom, brushed out my hair and applied powder to my face, to leave the house spic and span. There was Kyran, standing in front of... Goodness gracious no, a Chopper machine. Me on a motorbike? Unthinkable. I had never been on one before. Hopefully this wouldn't be too embarrassing.

"No worries, nothing can go wrong. This thing is usually quite safe. And I've had my license for seven years without an accident." He handed me a helmet. I looked from it to the chopper and back. I had to admit to myself that the machine did look really good. It was mainly silver and the seats were wide enough, too. So, in order to not be the spoilsport, I hauled the thing onto my head. Everything went muffled and my sight was a little limited as well. Somewhat sceptical I got on. Kyran started the motor and... waited. He tried to   (55) turn around, which was made difficult by the helmet. He muttered something I couldn't quite make out, as everything was so muffled. Only the second time around and with gestures, or rather, him demonstratively grabbing my hand and placing it on his hip, did I understand. Somewhat flustered I got it. I had to hold on somewhere. I held on reluctantly and very lightly. The motor howled once and Kyran took off. I have to admit that I was really scared, but it wasn't that bad after all. At first I tried not to grab him too forcefully in an attempt to show reserve, but when Kyran took one and then another turn, my grip grew tighter. Even though he didn't say anything, I thought I felt a slight flinch. Which was not surprising. My fingernails were digging into his T-shirt. Only after a few miles I rested my hands flat against his body. To be frank, I operated under the assumption that sitting on a motorbike would instinctively enhance the feeling of freedom, but so far that aspect was remaining hidden to me. Apparently I just hadn't unlocked the right sense for it yet, which, so I hoped, would come later. I also had no idea where we were headed. I didn't dare lift my head. I was too afraid that I would be unable to keep up in a turn, causing my body to move into the opposite direction and making us spin out of control. By now my bottom was starting to hurt as well. The streets he picked were not graced with smooth tarmac.

The sun was slowly coming out more and more, burning on my black leather jacket. This could only get more embarrassing. If we stopped anywhere, I would be covered in sweat stains. By now I didn't really care about anything anymore. Sure, I always had emergency deodorant and perfume on me, but no replacement blouse, not to mention the sweat stains between my legs. Not that I was excited, but to spend several miles sitting with spread legs on the leather seat of a Chopper motorbike while wearing skintight jeans, I don't know, it just had to go wrong. Shame-fuelled sweat was pouring down my forehead underneath the helmet. I didn't know how much longer we would be driving, but I had to admit to myself that I had had enough for the day. If we didn't stop soon I couldn't make guarantees for anything, least of all my mood. I tried to somehow find a better position and squirmed around, which Kyran sadly noticed. He called through his helmet to me.

"Not much longer and we're there." Embarrassing again. So I only nodded with a smile and tried to give him a thumbs up. I don't know if it worked, because my hands were tingling so much that they had fallen asleep. Hopefully I would be able to free myself from the hug later, otherwise he had to think I was eleven short of a dozen. Nonetheless he turned out to be right. A few miles down the road he slowed down.   (57)

For now I still couldn't raise my head, but from the corners of my eyes I saw that we were in a town. An old one. Sadly I couldn't spot a town sign, but we drove a bit further through the town until we reached a slight hill. The road curved and twisted as if we were in the deepest Sauerland, and we finally stopped. Kyran took off his helmet and I realized that he was a little sweaty as well. So I took mine off, too, and tried my best to get off the bike. Up here a brisk breeze blew Kyran's locks right back out of his face. I was similarly glad for the wind and let it blow through my sweat-soaked hair. Then I shook my hair out and lifted it off my neck, which immediately made me feel better. A bit self-conscious, I stood next to the Chopper, since I was afraid sweat may have run down my trousers. Thankfully this was not the case, I had only imagined it, and I breathed a sigh of relief. I also took off my coat to air it, and Kyran did the same. Contours were visible on his clothing because of the sweat, something that thankfully didn't apply to my white blouse. In an unobserved moment I could take the opportunity to use my deodorant. Oh, how good that felt. Now I was somewhat presentable again. We had stopped on top of a hill and were standing in front of a castle ruin. From here it did look enormous, but I didn't understand. Was he playing the tourist guide now? Well, I was willing to see what he wanted to show me. So I grinned, just like him.

(58)

"And what happens next?" I asked him. Kyran shook his head and motioned for me to follow him. Alright, I thought and followed him. We went to the entrance into the ruins, an old iron gate which was standing open for all the world. Then a stone path led upwards, bordered with grass along the sides. Half-crumbled stone walls poked out of the ground and a large building appeared. Ruined, but at least it had walls. Kyran crossed a small courtyard to reach another building, which was a kind of round tower with a steep staircase that was definitely leading up. Did he really want to go up there? I felt like I was in the scene from Highlander in which Connor McCloud is chased up the tower which is open on all sides and threatens to fall apart with every step. What if he was luring me up only to, whoops, push me down the stairs? Goodness gracious, Elara, you're seeing things. The young man did not appear tired in the slightest, he kept climbing higher and higher. The round staircase seemed to be endless, until I couldn't see Kyran anymore. Oh, whatever, I thought. I would have loved to turn straight around, but my legs were hurting so much and I didn't want to look weak. Get it together, I reprimanded myself and kept climbing higher. Some segments were pretty gloomy, since they had intact walls, and in others, like in a tunnel, I could see the light. My breath came faster and faster and I could hardly breathe. After a couple of seconds could I go on. At the end of the (59) staircase I could already feel a soft breeze. Fresh, salty air blew in my direction and I was eager to find out where it was coming from. My feet had reached the last step and a crown of light courted me with a grinning Kyran. He stood there, leaning against a wall that was stretching across the yard like a bridge. However, it didn't go much further. At the end of the bridge the wall had collapsed and scaffolding was constructed there. I usually was desperately afraid of heights and barely dared to go further, but Kyran held out his hand.

"No worries, the walls have been around since the 16th century. They will not collapse today of all days. Come on," he said.

I avoided taking his hand. That seemed too cowardly and I didn't want to admit my fear. So I pulled myself together and carefully peeked over the wall. Not just the air, but also the view were taking my breath away. Feeling a bit shaky, I tried to grab onto the balustrade for support. My knees were shaking, but I wanted this view. My hands slowly pulled me up and I could see the whole extent of beauty and nature. I almost forgot to breathe again. The view was spectacular. A flat, green, undulating landscape stretched out before me. Further away an azure blue peeked through. The sea was mirroring the land like in a picture. A sound escaped my   (60) throat that even I didn't recognise and I didn't even notice Kyran's face, which was staring at me in a kind of surprise.

"Isn't it?" he said. I couldn't turn my gaze away from the beauty of my surroundings and the view. "I sometimes come up here to turn off for a while. I mean, up here I can completely let go. No people, no noise, just…"

"Peace," I finished his sentence, and he repeated it softly. "Peace." Then he looked out across the sea, and his eyes seemed to shine just as much as mine. Oh, I was such a crybaby, it was embarrassing, but Kyran either didn't notice or simply ignored it. So we stood like this for a while and enjoyed the moment. I closed my eyes and absorbed the scent of salt and wind. Mingling with the green grass and hay it resulted in a wonderful mix of freedom, nature, and warmth. I had to admit that I hadn't felt this good in ages. Even Kyran next to me was forgotten. Only when he spoke I flinched and started swaying, so I held on to a stone block, which turned out to be quite wobbly in itself and was ripped half out of the wall. Kyran could only just hold on to me. The stone fell over the balustrade with a crash and I had to swallow and quickly see if I had hit anyone. But the mere view down made me feel dizzy. I hated the height, but the view was phenomenal. My hands were holding on to somewhere on my own body, and I had to find that Kyran's hands similarly were still holding me. Embarrassed and flushed deep red I looked at him.   (61)

For the first time I really noticed his eyes. Goodness gracious, I was getting even more red. He stared at me with a smile. Those gray-green eyes bored into mine. I quickly turned away and instead peeked down again.

"Don't worry, there is nobody down there you could have bludgeoned. Nothing happened. Look!" He motioned for me to come closer to the wall. My doubts were still pretty big. Internally, I tried to get a handle on my shaking. With lowered eyes and half upright I robbed closer to the wall. I felt like throwing up. I had tried to loosen his grip, but he didn't let go.

"Goodness gracious, why didn't you say so right away?" he said and pulled me straight back to the inner wall. Of course I stared at him stupidly.

"What? What... should I have said?" I wheezed more than I said. God, this was embarrassing. I wanted the earth to swallow me.

"You are afraid of heights!" he said dryly, but it sounded anything but amused. So I shrugged. Why would that concern him, anyway.

"I didn't know you had such a phobia, otherwise I wouldn't have had the idea to come here. Would you like to go back down? I think it would be better. I have some strong tea in my backpack. Come on, it will do you good", he commanded and I had no objections. (62)

It was hard to leave this view behind, but I wouldn't have been able to stand being up here with him any longer. In addition, more and more tourists were showing up. No wonder, the sun was slowly coming out and it was before noon. Everyone was sightseeing now to lay siege to the local pubs later.

It was hellishly difficult to get back down the stairs. As I said, tourists arrived in hordes at the ruins. No wonder, the view was simply fantastic. Nonetheless the stairs were not exactly made for several people. A somewhat heavy set man stormed straight up the stairs without concern for other people. His huffing came ever closer and my panic got worse. There was nothing that I could hold on to, much less avoid him. My pulse was racing. So I tried my best to squeeze myself flat against the wall. Just in time. The sweaty man stormed closer to me. He pushed me aside in a way that made me lose my footing on a step and I stumbled. This couldn't really be happening. Passed away in Ireland in an old ruin, run over by a sweaty tourist. Great prospects. Internally I said my last prayers, but a hand just managed to keep me from the abyss. Kyran nearly dislocated my arm when he held onto me and pushed the heavy set man aside. The guy only huffed and stared at him angrily, with his sandwich in his hand. Kyran growled something at him in Irish and pulled me down the stairs, holding my hand. Once we reached the ground he   (63) was now huffing as well. Partly from anger, partly from exertion. He ran a hand through his hair, then he leaned against the motorbike and took a deep breath.

"Such nonsense!" he thundered. I for one was still too busy shaking to reply.

"This is just typical. As soon as they get to this country, people have to behave like the last tourists. I… Oh, are you alright?" he asked, and I could only nod shakily. My hand hurt terribly and it was pretty red. The young man only noticed it now and took my hand again. He turned and flipped it like a schnitzel. Then he rummaged around in his backpack and bandaged my hand with some wound dressing. His hands were soft and warm. Oh, come on, El, I thought, how can you pay attention to something like that now.

I quickly pulled my hand away and just mumbled. "Thanks! It's all better already." Still, Kyran was a bit beside himself.

"This is so typical. I should have known that they would barge in here like so much cattle. I am so sorry to have brought you up here, especially since you are afraid of heights." He hit the seat of his bike lightly with his fist. I gratefully took a sip of his tea, which was hot in my throat but felt incredibly good. From up high we could hear the tourists call out all in a tumble, foremost the sweaty man, from whom bits of sandwich were falling down. From "Aah" to "Ooh" everything was represented, including "Mum, I am hungry. Mum, I need to pee." Which was an understatement.

"You couldn't have known. I mean, about my fear of heights," I said gloomily. He looked at me and nodded silently. "It was a really good idea. I have never seen such a view before. I... just want to say thank you for this trip," I added dejectedly, but I really meant it. He now looked at me for a moment, and it seemed to me like he was considering something. Then he grabbed his helmet and mine and handed it to me.

"Would you be up for another trip?" he asked and looked at me excitedly. I just nodded and demonstratively put my helmet back on. Just before we left, he half-looked back at me one more time.

"I don't know if it'll be your thing, but people say the view is even more marvellous than here," he said.

I could only reply sarcastically. "Well, if there are no walls and heights, I'm in." The look on his face was great. Should I really assume that there would be heights involved after all?

"Well, heights, yes, but no walls. Just wait and see. You can leave at any time." He winked at me a little and off we went. Past the old ruin we went back to the country road. Again I had no visibility in the helmet and could therefore only see slight outlines. After all, I was still kind of scared to ride along on this and did not dare to move my head or open my eyes. I also noticed that Kyran wasn't driving as fast anymore, which was no surprise. I could hardly hold on to him. Using only one hand I held on to Kyran's body, while the other one still pulsed horribly. After several miles the wind got stronger and my nose recognised an even stronger scent of salt. Were we back at the seafront? I meant to take a peek, but after a few potholes Kyran finally stopped. I took off my helmet and it hit me with a vehemence. The wind immediately took my breath away. I had to turn my back to the wind for a moment to get my breath back, and only now I realised that we were on top of a cliff that was protruding far into the ocean. It took my breath away. The cliffs were covered in green grass and small walls. These partly decorated the edges of properties and were partly used to keep nature somewhat at bay. As soon as I turned around, I turned my head slightly downwards to avoid the worst blast of wind on my face. This worked. The view was beyond words.

Vastness, unending vastness stretched out before me. It was to die for. Oh, please no, I thought and already my tears (66) were flowing again. Not just because of the beauty, the wind was also biting into my eyes. But here and now I didn't care. I almost felt like Scarlett O'Hara in "Gone With The Wind", falling to her knees in reverence and thanking God. I similarly sunk to my knees and sighed heavily. In the meantime, Kyran had wandered to the edge of the cliff and was enjoying the beauty from there.

I for my part could not help myself and lay down in the grass. It was as soft as eiderdown, and when I pressed my ear to the ground I could hear the roaring of the sea directly below me, the way the waves crashed against the rocks. It was gigantic and magical at the same time. One with nature, I allowed myself to unwind. It felt so good. I had completely lost track of time until Kyran came over and sat down next to me. When he spoke, I flinched a little.

"Where do you find all the energy for this?" he asked and looked at me. I blinked against the sun and raised myself onto my elbows.

"What do you mean?" I asked and pulled at a blade of grass. I was pretty relaxed, I thought.

"Well, the way you view things, I mean. You… you see things like… Don't take this the wrong way, but you see things (67) like a child that has seen the ocean for the first time." He smiled and I somehow found it cute. Oh please, Elara, don't be silly, this is just his shtick, I thought.

"Well, for someone like you this is probably nothing grand. I mean, you grew up here and know it all. I only know this from holidays by the north sea. Nothing against the north sea. It's an amazing place, but here… I don't know, everything here is even greener, cleaner, more magical. Even if this sounds kitsch and I sound like a small child, but that's how it is. I can't help being swept away by the nature around here."

Kyran was now also playing with a blade of grass. Now and again he was gazing out across the sea. "You know, it's not really easy to impress me, but there are people that fascinate me because they, like you, admire the nature here so much. Most tourists that come here hardly spare it a glance. They just want to see everything they can in one day, quick, quick. But you can't explore something like this quickly. Something like this has to sink in, that's why I brought you here. I mean, when I saw you for the first time in the garden, I knew that you felt something that others can't." He stopped speaking and silence fell. I didn't know what this was supposed to be. Would I be able to trust him? And if so, what were his intentions?

"Believe me, I am not usually like this. I can be quite different, but as I said, I've never seen anything like this. Can I ask you something anyway?" I glanced at him from the side and Kyran simply nodded. "Why did you do it? I mean, in the beginning, to use this other guy. You could have just said that you don't want to do it and everyone would have been fine with it," I said.

Kyran squirmed a little. He was visibly uncomfortable. Nonetheless he held my gaze, which was starting to make me feel awkward.

"Well, as I said, my manager said it was a good idea. We had planned it to be the last time this year. I have actually been against it for a while now, but before I could say anything the competition had already gone online. You know, most people who won the competition in the past kept wanting to prove something to me. It got worse and worse as the so-called fans got more intrusive. They ambushed me, didn't even stop at my parents' house. That's why I didn't want to do this anymore, but when I saw you sitting there like that... I don't know, but somehow my belief came back to me. I know it sounds a bit silly." He looked at me with a smile, before he went straight back to questioning me.

(69)

"What made you compete here in the first place?" he wanted to know. I swallowed a little. Should I tell him the truth? I tossed my blade of grass and twisted my fingers.

"Well, I am one of those stupid tourists." I laughed when I saw the moment of embarrassment on his face. But I continued speaking. "No, really. I don't know. I mean, sure, I admit that your music struck a chord with me, but when I heard of this competition all I wanted was to go to Ireland. It was my chance, but I didn't take it." I had to laugh as I said it. Kyran didn't understand.

"But you're here now," he said. I had to think. Should I make up a new version or just tell the truth? That made me laugh even more. "What?" he asked. "What's so funny?" he repeated. I shook my head until I had calmed down a little.

"Alright, fine, I… Well, I fell asleep on my computer keyboard and in the morning I had joined the raffle. I even still had the letters imprinted on my cheek. I am so sorry, it's nothing against you, but when I found myself on the ship and we landed in the harbour I was glad that fate wanted this for me." I laughed again and covertly glanced at him. Did he believe me or did he think I was lying? At least I knew that it was the truth.

"You're serious?" he asked and looked at me with a mixture of amusement and shock. But I could only laugh. In doing so, I sat up and stretched out my arms. Then I ran across the grass to the cliff's edge, where I stopped carefully. I stood with my back to the sea and started running. Like a kite attempting to fly, I wanted the wind to carry me. It pressed into my back and I almost managed it. My feet got lighter and lighter. Too light, perhaps. A few feet further down my flight attempts came to an abrupt end. I stumbled and fell into the grass, which caught me in a soft embrace. I quickly turned around and looked into Kyran's face. He didn't understand and I laughed again.

"Oh, I am sorry, but have you never done this before? Let the wind carry you and pretend with each gust that you can fly? You should try it some time."

Completely out of breath I lay back down in the grass and stretched out my arms and legs. To savour the moment like this was like magic. My eyes closed and I enjoyed the moment. As I did, a shadow flew over my face, and when I opened my eyes I looked into Kyran's face, which was bent over mine. His fingers pulled a blade of grass out of my hair and he flicked it awkwardly to the side, but he stayed sitting where he was. He glanced at me.

"See, this is exactly what fascinates me about people. There aren't many like you. Who accept this countryside like that. Who are so... yes, so unique. It's remarkable. You are remarkable," he said and looked at me again. A shiver ran through me and I wanted to sit up. But as soon as I propped myself up, my wrist gave way and I flinched away from the pain. I cursed the idiot tourist. Kyran himself was quickly all gentleman and held me.

"Not too bad. I'm fine," I said with a grimace, but Kyran kept holding me. He took my hand and massaged it lightly, and he stared at me so piercingly that I felt hot and cold at the same time. His face came closer and closer, and before I knew it his lips rested on mine as softly as dew. First like a piece of paper, so hesitantly and softly, but then the kiss intensified. His tongue tried, softly but demandingly, to gain access to my mouth. I didn't know if I should let it happen, but my body decided differently. Hesitantly at first, but then with abandonment I opened my mouth and allowed his tongue to play with mine. My head was spinning and I did not understand what was happening. It seemed like we spent hours in the kiss, but in reality it was mere seconds. Somewhat embarrassed, we separated. Considering that I didn't like him, due to his arrogant behaviour, I seemed very happy to let myself be kissed by him. Still quite confused (72) and a little ashamed I turned away. What was I even doing? I asked myself. I was a middle-aged woman, divorced, and now this, smooching like a teenager with a young man I hardly knew. Of course I could already hear Ellis say, "Yes, great, you are finally coming out of your shell. Take him, he looks fabulous. You owe it to yourself. And especially Mike." Oh God, Mike. If he were to find out I was a goner. Colour rose to my cheek, but Kyran slowly came closer and held on to my hand. I looked at him innocently, but I must have seemed quite caught out.

"What worries you?" he asked and looked at me intensely with his grey-green eyes. I didn't want to look at him, but I couldn't help myself.

"I… it's just… oh, I just don't know if this is right. You… You… well, you hardly know me. Why…?" I asked, but Kyran came closer again and kissed me. Then he smiled at me.

"You are a person who still surprises me. I mean, when I saw you for the first time I only thought of the silly tourists. Forgive me, but when I then saw you in the garden I knew that you are different, somehow. Your presence and your feel for this island are simply magical. I have never experienced this in a person before." What should I do, I thought, maybe just smile.   (73)

But I didn't feel entirely comfortable. He pulled me back to the Chopper by the hand.

"Come on, I have another little idea. How to you feel about food? Dublin has a rustic little pub with the best burgers and chicken."

I shrugged. To show my support, I added, "And Guinness!", then I was laughing as well and we drove off again. This time the ride was more relaxed and I could hold on more gently, although I had no idea where this would end. I wasn't actually hungry, but I hadn't had much food today either. Although I remembered to wonder what was going on with Rachel. What would she think, and wouldn't it be unfair to her? At the next stop I would talk to him about it for sure.

Chapter Five

The curving and swerving was starting to grow on me. The wind was finding its way into my helmet and every gap it could fit through. I also tried to raise my head more and to look more intensively at my surroundings, but without letting go of Kyran. We were driving on the motorway and therefore, there was sadly not much to see. There wasn't much apart from bushes and the occasional storehouse or sign. But when we entered Dublin, it was brimming with life. Beginning with the expensive suburbs of houses in neat rows, which gave way to stores and shops and garages, as well as shopping centres and pubs. We kept driving on all the way to famous O'Connell Street. Here one shop bordered on the next. Everything was there, from Starbucks Coffee to Burger King to Subway and the little Spar supermarkets. We crossed the Penny Bridge and turned into Temple Bar Street. This was *the* pub quarter par excellence. On weekends it was filled with a riot of life. Even more so in the summer, of course, so today was a comparatively quiet day. Somewhere near Temple Bar Street, Kyran stopped in front of a rustic pub with brown stone walls and flower boxes in the windows. A small table with two chairs stood in front of the entrance. I had no idea if it was for sitting or merely decoration.   (75)

Maybe it was just the smoking zone. Anyway, as soon as Kyran came in the door the innkeeper greeted him exuberantly. He had to be a regular. Which was no surprise. Outside was a sign saying that this pub had live music every night. Of course, Kyran was a singer and probably spent a lot of time here. A few guests were already there. Three men were sitting at the bar,chatting loudly, and from time to time one of them would bellow out laughter and they would clap each other on the shoulders, then clink glasses. An older couple was sitting by the window, eating chicken and chips. On the opposite side sat a young couple who were eating a burger. These two looked more like students to me. Both had their books open and were discussing it between ketchup and a coke. My young company had a quick chat with the innkeeper and came back with two glasses of Guinness. The menu was quite small, but he promised that this pub had the best burger and chicken, so I picked a burger. While we waited for the food, I drank my first beer on tap in Ireland. Goodness gracious, this is good, I thought and licked the foam from my lips. Kyran grinned at me again.

"What?" I asked, a little embarrassed. He grinned.

"See, this is exactly why I like you. You make it a joy of a lifetime to enjoy even a Guinness. That's fantastic and incredible at the same time." He squeezed my hand, and (76)

I felt somehow comfortable, not to say domestic. We chatted about his home and his parents, who lived here and had a small knife shop. Of course his father was already retired, but little Kyran hadn't felt like taking over the shop so far. His ambitions went more in the direction of Irish music, and he stayed on that track. Which wasn't exactly without success, either. He had made a name for himself, even off the island, far across the ocean. Now it was my turn to speak. Should I really tell him all about Mike? I preferred to put my cards on the table over false pretenses. So I told him everything, from beginning to end. Somewhat sheepish silence fell after Kyran told me of his ex-wife, a marriage that hadn't held because of drug problems on her side. Since then Kyran had had his own problems with women.

By now it was late in the evening. Dusk was breaking and Kyran wanted to stay some more, maybe to play a small gig as well. For my part, I felt a little uncomfortable. I had been in this clobber all day and wished for a shower and fresh clothes.

As if he could read my thoughts, Kyran just said, "How about I take you home first, then you can freshen up some and we will see each other again later. If you'd like?" he asked me. I only nodded, but then I remembered Rachel again.

"What about Rachel, by the way? I mean, she's probably going to be really mad if she sees me driving off with you, even though she won the ticket just as much as I did."

He laughed again. "Oh, I think she is in good hands, as far as I can tell." He winked at me and I could have immediately flung my arms around his neck, but I didn't. Right after we drove off we stopped at a lay-by on the way to the hut. A few benches made from tree trunks were standing around with a view over a large lake. It was fantastic. It should really have stood out to me when we were first brought to the hut. Well, perhaps there were different streets there, or I had been in too much internal turmoil. Kyran sat down on one of the trunks and looked out over the lake.

"Come here, sit down a moment." He held out his hand for me and I sat down next to him. He was definitely right. The view was amazing, even though dusk was already approaching. I could almost imagine us being by Loch Ness and Nessie was about to come straight out of the water. The water was so deep and dark and yet mystical, surrounded by mother nature, located right by a motorway. And yet it somehow radiated calm and something of fairyland. Oh, please, Elara, you're getting sentimental. But I couldn't turn my head away. I got goosebumps, not from the cold, but from the beauty. It was truly fantastic. Kyran looked at me and only nodded.   (78)

He was still holding my hand and stroked it with his fingers. It tingled and I could have melted. The water was still, only when a bird made its rounds a small wave lapped at the shore. Even if the occasional car drove past, it did not take away from the beauty. Just when the sun was slowly setting, the light put an orange film over the lake's surface like in a movie. It looked phenomenal and all that was missing were pixies and gnomes. Kyran's body was right behind me and I felt his warmth intensely. My pulse was racing a bit. When he kissed me softly on the neck, I started shivering. I could have abandoned myself to the moment, but a couple of motorbike freaks disturbed our togetherness. Just like us, they were taking a break. One of the drivers took a can of beer out of his bag and the other was bellowing something. Kyran seemed a little annoyed.

"Come, let's go!" he said and got up. I was similarly reluctant to separate myself from him, but considering the motorbikers it seemed to be a hint of fate. So we went back to the house I inhabited. I was surprised to find Sean's car still parked in front of it. Kyran turned off his motor.

"See, I told you that your Rachel is taken care of," he grinned and pointed at the car. I only understood slowly, although my brain was working on it until I got it.

"You mean Rachel and Sean?" I asked and Kyran was already nodding.

"Didn't you know or see that? I thought it was evident." He softly kissed my neck again and I turned around to him. His eyes bored into mine and I could have lost myself in them. But again our togetherness was not meant to be. Sean had apparently heard the Chopper and was coming outside, looking somewhat sheepish. But he was laughing impishly and I could see Rachel in the window, who was just wiping chocolate from her mouth. She was grinning as well.

"Oh, that late already," Sean said and quickly got into his car. Kyran similarly gave me his hand, gallantly kissed mine and made a break for it.

"I'll come pick you up in an hour," he whispered just before he left and I only nodded. If I only knew where we were going, I thought, it would probably be advantageous for my wardrobe.
"And, did you have a nice day?" Rachel purred and looked at me dreamily. I could only nod and went directly to the shower. Next door I could still hear the loud music from Rachel, who was watching her much-loved MTV channel. I actually felt pretty annoyed by that, but I was floating in clouds so high that it made me dizzy. Nonetheless I tried to get ready quickly. I washed myself, did my hair and got dressed.   (80)

My choice fell on a short, black dress with lace trimmings, with it I wore black boots and my leather jacket. I had twisted my hair into curls and put on discreet make-up. I didn't like to tart myself up too much. My motto was that if I was walking around all sexy, discreet make-up was enough. Yes, I was happy with myself. I quickly grabbed a glass of red wine and drained it in one go. Rachel had also gotten changed and grinned at me.

"Well, this is going to be exciting. A live concert with Kyran" she said and made herself a sausage sandwich. Mentally, I was quite tense. How would I react to Kyran when he came to pick us up?

The evening approached and I waited in front of the door for our company. They appeared promptly around the corner. It was the old Mustang again and as soon as I saw Rachel's grin I knew that Sean was sitting in the driver's seat. He got out and held the door open like a gentleman. Rachel stormed past me like a steamroller and immediately got into the passenger seat. All I had left was the backseat.

Sean held the door open for me and quickly whispered "He is waiting for you in the pub" and laughed. I had no idea what to think, but I accepted it. After all, I only had two days left here. So we took off and I watched as Sean flirted with Rachel. (81)

That sure was amusing. They seemed made for each other after all. Apparently they had the same conversation topics. No idea, maybe food or whatever.

We went to the pub in the cradle of Dublin and were immediately led to a table by the stage. It was still in the process of being built, but not a trace of Kyran. Once the last person had built up his drum, I felt a whisper of air on my neck and a soft kiss was placed on it. Kyran was there and the crowd was roaring. It was amazing as always. From beginning to end I listened to his voice and Rachel was similarly completely smitten. Of course we would never be good friends, but I was a little glad to know her. At least I wasn't so alone here. The waiter brought us two Guinness at the behest of Kyran. My roommate didn't really like it, it was too bitter for her. So she pushed the glass in my direction and ordered herself a glass of wine.

The evening was getting long. Kyran did not finish his session until after eleven, maybe half eleven. He quickly got changed and made his way to us after numerous autographs. He also ordered a Guinness and downed it in one go. Sean sat down next to Rachel and she immediately started giggling. Kyran stealthily grabbed my hand under the table and I flushed bright red right away. His chair came closer and closer and I could feel his warm body next to me. The other   (82) band members came over and greeted us warmly with a glass of whiskey, which Rachel could sadly not stomach. She needed some fresh air and Sean happily accompanied her. He quickly offered to take her home. Kyran just nodded and to be honest I had no idea how I would get home, but Kyran was all gentleman. He nodded towards me.

"No worries, I'll take you home in a bit," he said and one of his friends clapped the lead singer's shoulder.

"Well, ready for a game? Winner gets a Jameson," said Dyllon, one of his band buddies. He held a bunch of darts under Kyran's nose and pointed at his glass of Jameson Whiskey. Kyran just shrugged his shoulders and looked at me.

"Why not," I said. To be honest I had never played dart before, but hey, I was on holiday and couldn't do more than make an embarrassment of myself. So all systems go. First Dyllon aimed the darts, then Marcus, another member of the band, and Gerard, then it was my and Kyran's turn. He bent over to me.

"Do you even know how to play dart?" he asked me, but I had to admit I didn't. I felt awkward.

"Oh, I… I played a bit in the past, just for fun, but I'm afraid I'm pants at it. Maybe I should pass." My anxious gaze got stuck on the darts, but Kyran merely grinned and pressed them into my hand.

"Whatever," he said. Fine, I thought and took up the darts. I had to stand a bit to the side and raised my arm. I didn't feel good about this, especially because the others were making jokes along the lines of she's never played and typical woman. What the hell, I thought and launched away. The laughter from the beginning turned into a shocked oh, how... and Dyllon stared at me, while Kyran burst out laughing.

"Goodness gracious, you told me she can't play?" Dyllon thundered. I had no idea what I did. Innocently, I met Kyran's eyes, but he just nodded.

"Don't worry. You're sure you've never played before?" he asked me as well. I truthfully shook my head. Pure dumb luck. If it were up to Dyllon I would have been excluded right away, but as time went on the game got more fun. The whiskey flowed on my side, as it did on Dyllon's. Kyran held back a bit after a while. He still had to drive and I felt a little bit guilty, since I didn't know how I would get back. At one point, when I was turned away a bit and tossed some darts with Marcus, I heard Dyllon and Kyran whisper to each other. (84)

"She really is a super woman, where did you get her... I mean... How did you get to her?" But Kyran just shook his head and looked at me. I felt somehow caught out, but I gave it my all and showed myself from my best side. Which, as I found, worked quite well. Kyran's eyes never left mine again and Dyllon was similarly a little astonished.

"You really made a good choice. Say, is this something serious?" he asked and looked at his friend. Kyran glanced back at him. He only shrugged and grinned again. I gave it my all and threw darts with all I had. Tonight I was inarguably the queen. I felt amazing and the whiskey did its part. The evening got longer and the bar emptier. It was the middle of the week and tonight wasn't as busy as usual, but in my opinion that made it all the more fun. For me the evening had been a success. After even Dyllon had excused himself with gritted teeth, Kyran and I also made our way out. He was here with his Chopper again. I actually had some doubts regarding riding it. Especially considering my dress, but I only laughed and pulled it up as far as it would go, sitting down with the words "As long as nobody sees".

Kyran swallowed and grinned at me. "Sure, if you say so." He quickly pressed a kiss to my cheek and started the motor. (85)

No sooner had we taken off that he slapped his helmet and turned to me.

"Would you mind if we made a quick detour to my place?" he asked. Should I be on my guard, like, was this an attempt at seduction? I was a bit unsure, I hadn't had a man since Mike. Be it for kissing or anything else.

As if he could read my thoughts, Kyran replied immediately. "Oh, not what you are thinking. Goodness gracious, no. I actually forgot to feed my dog, yes, another one of my secrets. You can wait outside if you want. It's really just a quick scoop of food," he said and looked at me honestly. Dogs! Hmm, I really didn't care for dogs, I was more partial to cats, but okay, if he was just going to quickly feed him or her. Okay.

"Okay, no problem. I'll wait then. Erm, what kind of dog do you have?" I asked. I shouldn't have asked. He immediately pulled out a picture of a large golden retriever. By and large I didn't mind big dogs so much, but I didn't really like them either. Nonetheless I nodded in agreement. So we took off again, only to stop at the end of Dublin in a quiet suburb. It was a pretty, but simple terrace house with a front yard, typically Irish. A small drive led up to a green plank door,   (86) separated from the street by a garden fence. As soon as we stopped I noticed barking coming from inside. Kyran took off his helmet and indicated that he would only be a few minutes. Of course I nodded and got off as well. I also took off my helmet and waited until Kyran had disappeared inside the house. In the neighbourhood I could hear a TV and an old man with a hat came towards me. He greeted me in Irish and walked on muttering to himself. A light breeze blew a strand of hair out of my face. Suddenly the door opened and Kyran was calling out to me.

"Careful, he got loose! I am sorry, but he's been alone too long," he complained and ran after his dog. But the animal was faster and ran directly towards me. Before I could react, the beast of an animal was panting at me. He licked me all over and I couldn't help but pet him. I laughed out loud and saw Kyran's gaze rest on my face. He was truly fascinated.

"What… I mean, he usually never has this much trust in a stranger. He… usually doesn't like strangers. This is really remarkable," he added and came toward us.

"What's his name, anyway?" I asked and scratched the dog behind the ears, which he seemed to enjoy.

"Jimmy! His name is Jimmy." Kyran also scratched the dog's ears, and the dog lay down flat on the ground and on his back so that we could pet his paunch. I had to laugh and Kyran was also positively surprised. "I don't recognise this from him at all. As I said, he usually doesn't like strangers, but here... I say," he said amazed. Like two family members we hung around with the dog and took turns petting him. But my bladder was demanding my attention.

I stuttered. "I... erm, can I please use your bathroom for a second? I think I had too much Guinness," I grinned. While I said it I slowly shifted my weight from one leg to the other and Kyran laughed.

"Of course. Come on, I'll show you. Jimmy, come inside!" he told the dog, who was following his command. Kyran took the lead, put some doggie bones into Jimmy's bowl, which the dog immediately began to gnaw on, and directed me down the hallway. The decor was spartan. The entrance led straight into the lounge area. A large sofa adorned the room along the window, as well as a table made of light wood, and on the wall in front of it were a television and a light-coloured bookshelf full of document folders and some books. On one side was a bar with a kitchen behind it. A short hallway led to the bedroom and the toilet. I quickly went in. (88)

Damn, that was really embarrassing. But the Guinness was really pressing down and I was relieved about the stop. No idea if I could have made it all the way to the holiday home. Either way, I was glad. I could hear Kyran chat to Jimmy a little as he gave him the food. I had taken off my leather jacket and was carrying it over one arm. As soon as I came out of the bathroom, Kyran asked me, "Well, how about a glass of red wine?", and I couldn't say no to that and accepted it gratefully. The glass in my hand, I looked at the pictures on the wall, which showed Kyran in younger years with who I presumed to be his father, fishing and in a pub. That made me laugh. Like father, like son, I thought. As soon as I was standing here, Jimmy came over to me. He panted at me and wanted to be petted. I bent down and did so. Kyran looked at us both. He seemed to be in a different world. After a while I got back up to prevent my legs from falling asleep and briefly leant against the shelf, which was next to me. As soon as I turned around, Kyran was standing in front of me. He put his hands against the shelf I was leaning against. He took the glass from my hands and put it on the shelf, then he came closer and lay his lips gently but demandingly on mine. His hand went more towards my neck and gently pulled me away from the shelf. I couldn't help but follow. We kept kissing along the corridor, until we reached a door, which he pushed open with his free hand. It was undoubtedly his bedroom.   (89)

A giant bed was standing in the middle of the room, made of light oak. Next to it were a large armoire and two sets of drawers. The decor was bright and inviting. The bedding was similarly made from a light-coloured satin. On the walls hung a few pictures of fishermen and old harbours, a small TV was standing by the window, which was open and let in a cool breeze. The white curtains curled lightly back and forth. We reached the bed still kissing and he gently put me down on it. When he did, he looked at me for a moment and I could feel his hot breath even more intensely. His pulse rose and so did mine. Again he took my face in his hands and kissed me passionately, while I was laying on the bed. He was laying right next to me. His shoes were half undone and his shirt was also partly unbuttoned. Was I really ready for this step? I wondered, but I already knew the answer. I didn't care. To hell with Mike, and to hell with my restraint. If not now, when? After all this would probably just be a one night stand and I would have to go back in two days. Kyran was laying on the bed and I looked at him. The black jeans and blue jean shirt looked drop-dead gorgeous on him. He turned to me so that I was now lying on top of him and looking at him. He took my head in his hands and kissed me again. In return, I kissed his throat and wandered down his open shirt with my lips. His pulse was racing. I continued kissing his chest. He moaned softly and sat up to quickly slip off his shirt. I also got rid of my   (90) dress, and, as opposed to him, I was now wearing only my bra and panties. Thank goodness I had dug out my black lace undies earlier, since I had found that they matched the dress. I kissed him again on the chest and worked my way towards his belt, fumbling with it until I had opened it. Kyran moaned a little louder and slipped off his jeans. I could see his manhood clearly and how erect he was. As I was about to try my hand on his underwear, he grabbed me and turned us around. Now I was on the bed and Kyran kissed every inch of my body. His fingers found my bra and undid it with ease. It was tossed aside and I was exposed. I was actually a little ashamed of my body. After all, I wasn't as young as I had been, and I tried to cover my breasts with my arms. But Kyran lifted them finger by finger and kissed me even more passionately. My fingers went to my mouth to prevent me from yelling with desire. I turned again and was now sitting on him while he kept covering me with his lips. He moaned softly.

"Please stay with me. Tonight," he whispered and kissed me again. I squirmed and arched my back, which let me feel his erection. Only a scrap of cloth was now preventing us from the actual act. Kyran held me so tightly that it made me moan. We turned again on the bed and the last pieces of clothing were tossed aside. I breathed in his scent and felt his hot breath on my neck. He kissed me more and   (91) more passionately, which I could also feel in his manhood. I sat on him with crossed legs and his manhood entered me. My thighs shivered and so did I. His head pressed against my chest and his lips covered me. My senses grew faint and I enjoyed every moment. We rocked under the influence of love. One wave chased the next to the climax. Exhausted, but happy we lay next to each other in the pillows. He spooned me from behind and held me safe. While the wind gently blew through the room, we fell asleep.

Only hours later I woke up with something wet on my face. My eyes had to adjust to the darkness in the room. After a few moments, I finally realised who was licking my hand. Jimmy! Oh, whatever, the bed was big enough. I got him on the bed and scratched his belly. He appreciated it with low grunts. Stretched out next to me, Jimmy fell asleep again. Kyran noticed and wanted to chase him off right away, but I grinned and left the dog on the bed, trying to keep Kyran's hands off him, which in turn motivated him to grab me instead. His mouth started kissing my neck and his hands worked their way down my body. First I had to laugh, but then I sank back into ecstasy and allowed his body to cover mine. His hands worked their way towards my centre, while his manhood inched closer to me. His fingers kept working and I moaned loudly, which made his breath come faster as well,   (92) and he entered me again. We drifted on the waves of pleasure until we reached the climax.

Two more hours later the sun carefully peeked in through the window, and Jimmy blissfully turned around. Kyran was breathing calmly now and still held me tightly in his arms. I for myself thought about taking a shower and secretly snuck out into the bathroom. Once there, I let the hot water run down my body and joyfully soaped myself down. I had forgotten to close the door and was a bit surprised to find Kyran appear next to me. He stood behind me and let the water pearl down his skin as well, while his hands touched my body and he kissed me. I turned around and passionately captured his mouth in mine, wandering down to the centre of his lust. I felt his erection. He gently held down my head and I took to him until he exploded in ecstasy. Exhausted, we hugged each other and let the hot water wash over our bodies. After a few minutes my skin was shrivelled and I had to get out of the shower. I quickly grabbed a towel and dried myself off, while Kyran continued his shower. The bathroom was completely fogged up, and I made my escape to brew some coffee. As soon as I was outside I could hear Kyran inside.

"Uhhh, hu... Wow!" he called out and laughed. By now I had gotten dressed and prepared a light breakfast. Kyran slowly stepped out of the bath, a grin threatening to split his face.(93)

He went into the bedroom and got dressed. Wearing fresh clothes, he walked towards me, gave Jimmy a quick scritch and then kissed me intensively. We both knew I had to go back soon, first of all to the holiday house to get changed. And yet, separation was looming. I hadn't meant to address it, but it was somehow on my mind.

"Listen, I… I have to get changed and you… you know I have to go back tomorrow," I said and looked down. Kyran turned away a little and looked out the window, then he turned towards me, took me in his arms and refused to let me go. He buried his face in my hair and held me protectively. I merely heard the hint of a whisper.

"Don't go! Please stay with me!" I heard. A shiver ran down my spine. What had happened here, what would happen now? I had no idea. After all, I couldn't simply stay here. I had nothing and nobody here, no job, no home or anything. And anyway, wasn't this all happening too fast? I didn't know. Of course I didn't want to leave. Everything was perfect. He was perfect.

Chapter Six

We stayed entwined like that for a while longer before we had to leave. Kyran quickly gave Jimmy his food and then we hopped on the Chopper. I put my arm around his waist and held on tight. My head was resting against his back and I breathed in his aftershave. We drove the distance to the holiday home in silence. When we got to the front door, Rachel was not in yet. She was out with Sean, who was wooing her and no mistake. Kyran got off and walked me to the house. Since it was the early morning, a light frost was covering the grass, bedewing it with a soft mist. Spiderwebs lay like spun sugar on the grass. Kyran led me to the garden and held on to my hand the entire time. I sighed and watched the small stream as it was burbling along. Everything was so quiet and idyllic. Kyran wrapped his arms around me from behind and rested his head on mine. He was so warm and his hands felt so protective. And yet time was ticking. The young man knew it and turned me around to face him. His eyes were glistening a little. Were they holding tears? Oh please no, I thought. I wanted to look away, but I could not manage it. His mouth came closer and his lips lay on mine. Was this the goodbye kiss now? I did not want it to be. And yet my plane was leaving soon. For a while, we stood tightly intertwined in the garden and lost all sense of time. Eventually, we only just noticed a car come up the road. It was Sean and Rachel. They were giggling and playing around. Kyran looked at me and I shrugged. It was time to separate. So we went hand in hand back to the house.

A call from Kyran's manager made him lose his composure. A photoshoot was still pending, and I knew that he had to comply. This day was meant to be only for me and my thoughts. Only in the evening we were supposed to go to a last concert with Kyran. I actually didn't want to go, but on the other hand I felt I had to. I ended up not seeing Rachel all day. She was having fun with Sean and to be honest, I really approved of it. They were a great match. Not that I had against portly women, but Sean was of the same kidney, rather chubby, with short, prickly hair and a bit of an oddball.

That evening Kyran's mood didn't seem to be the same, either. His songs sounded more melancholy and drifting. Even Dyllon noticed and glared at me. During a break I could hear him talk to Kyran.

"Goodness gracious, Kyran, forget her. She goes back to Germany and you'll find a better one for sure. Believe me, this is just the beginning. There's enough chicks out there to turn your head. Or was she that good in bed?" He laughed,   (96) but Kyran didn't seem to feel like laughing. He turned away a bit and saw me. Dyllon also looked at me and grinned. He was trying to drive a wedge between us. Of course I got that. A few minutes before Kyran had to go back on stage, Dyllon came over to me. He was holding a whiskey, which he handed to me, then he leaned closer and purred, "Listen, it's not good for him if he has such a distraction. I mean sure, if I had someone like you I'd be confused too, but hey, life goes on. I'm sorry, but it would really be better if you left and forgot about him. Put it down as an adventure and then no hard feelings." He grinned again and went back to his buddies. Was he right? When Kyran started singing again, I didn't feel so great anymore. How should this evening end? Would he just drop me off at home and that was that? It was probably for the best. The evening got longer, and when Kyran's performance was over, he made a beeline to me. In the background I could see Dyllon lurking and watching me punitively. I quickly looked away, but not without Kyran noticing.

"Let's go outside," he said and nodded at his band. One of them raised his glass at us and another just nodded. Kyran quickly grabbed two Guinness and pulled me along with him. I didn't know if drinking was the best solution at the time, but it seemed that way to me. On a ledge, he sat down and   (97) pulled me into his lap. He held me tight and buried his face in my shoulder. Neither of us could say anything. In the pub, the last cleaning was underway and the rest of the band was leaving for home as well. Only Dyllon was still standing in the door.

"Kyran!" he demanded, but Kyran refused to listen to him. "Kyran, we gotta go!" he demanded again.

I looked at the young singer and said shakily, "I guess this is goodbye," trying for a joke, but Kyran kept hold of me. He raised his face to mine and kissed me. My legs were shaking. A nervous knocking against the door showed me that Dyllon was getting more impatient.

"I think it... is better if you leave now. It's no use anyway. I mean, my flight leaves very early tomorrow morning," I whispered into his ear, but Kyran shook his head.

"No, no, please don't go. Stay with me tonight," he whispered back and kissed my neck. Oh, how happily I would follow the suggestion. But then what? I knew that this was how it had to be and end.

Dyllon knocked again and called for his friend. Then he was coming over to us and grinned widely. "I hate to interrupt (98) your sweet togetherness, but we still have to do the meeting for tomorrow. Sorry, sweetheart," he patted my shoulder. Kyran was now somewhat annoyed. He got up now and took me by the hand, raising a finger of his other hand to signal to Dyllon that he needed to be patient. The other man did not like that. He kicked a wine cork on the ground away with his foot and slammed his fist against the door. In the meantime Kyran pulled me further down the street. We walked down O'Connell Street until we reached the bridge crossing the Liffey, one of Dublin's rivers. Most people had already dispersed, only a few couples and the occasional drunk were around. Once more we sat down on a bench and the breeze came over from the river. Gently, yet cool, it lay a film of salt and smog on my forehead. Kyran looked at me intensely. I covertly turned around to see if Dyllon had followed us after all, but he was standing in the door to the pub and smoked, stalking up and down like a tiger.

"Well, now you have more time for your groupies again," I tried to cheer Kyran up. That didn't seem to be what he wanted to hear. He stood up now and ran his hands through his hair.

"Elara, why can't you stay? At least try!" he asked, yes almost begged me. I looked at him and he looked so lost. He wrapped his arms around me. He smelled so good and I (99) could feel his warmth. A cough from far away made me sit up. Kyran also turned around. It was Dyllon.

"Alright, alright. I'll be there soon. Why don't you go ahead?" Kyran offered, but Dyllon didn't want to.

He called out to us. "No worries, I can wait. You don't even have a car to get out of here. After all, this can't take that much longer." The last sentence was said in a low voice, and he was already playing with his car keys. I had completely forgotten that the lead singer was really dependent on his friend, since Sean had brought Rachel home already. There really was no point, I decided.

"Kyran, we… It's better this way. I'll take a taxi and you go to that meeting. We… we can chat on the phone some time," I said with a laugh and squeezed him one more time. This time I was the wedge. After all, it had to end somehow. Even if it killed me. My heart was racing so fast and I tried to somehow hold back my tears. To my relief, I had to admit that Dyllon was now really coming in handy. That way I didn't have to be embarrassed and could turn away to quickly wipe my eyes. Deep breaths, I thought and turned around again.

Dyllon looked quite annoyed, but he put up a brave front. "I really hate bothering you, but time really is ticking.   (100)

You can still say goodbye tomorrow morning. How about you go to the airport and I bring Kyran. What do you think?" he purred. His face was betraying his lies. This time I kissed Kyran, short but intense. For me this was goodbye, I knew as much, but for him?

"I will see you tomorrow morning. Promise!" he said and stopped a taxi for me. Another fleeting kiss and I was off. From the back seat I could just about still see Dyllon's triumphant grin. So that was it. My world fell apart and as soon as I got out of the car at the house the dam broke and I cried.

Chapter Seven

The whole damn night I could barely sleep. I woke up feeling like I had been run over by a truck and sporting a headache. I had already packed my things the evening before and only had to wash myself and get dressed. There was no time left for breakfast, as Sean was already by the door waiting to pick us up. Rachel grinned widely and Sean also looked somehow more relaxed. I looked around for a moment, but Sean shook his head. Kyran wouldn't come. Maybe it was better this way. While Rachel rode shotgun and chatted with Sean, I looked out at the nature that zoomed past us at high speeds. Despite all its beauty, I could not think anything at all. I felt empty. Less than ten miles along I already saw the first airport car parks. An Aer Lingus machine was just getting ready for landing. That had to be mine, or maybe not. I didn't care. My gaze fell on my phone every few seconds. I had messages, but not from Kyran. At least two dozen from Mike and Ellis. The clock ticked and ticked. Every car that reminded me even remotely of Kyran's made me perk up. But it was never him. Until the last second I had hoped he would come after all. Nothing! I was already feeling lucky that we went back on a plane and I didn't have to share cabins with Rachel again, not after this adventure. Our flight was called and Sean said   (102) goodbye to Rachel, who was exuberant. He only shrugged and looked at me with pity in his eyes. Should I say anything to him, give him a last message? No, I didn't. Instead I boarded the plane and within the next thirty minutes, we were off. On this flight I felt so ill that I wanted to spit, but I took a pill and all but floated home. At Cologne airport, however, the present hit me like a lightning bolt. Loud streets, stinking smog and unfriendly people, and yet throughout the big city I could hear that melody repeating in my head that could not be more Irish. Kyran's eyes were everywhere. My eyes filled with tears when I heard Ellis' voice call all the way across the terminal.

"Aaah, there you are again. Welcome, welcome!" she called towards me. Thank God that I had been able to convince her to come pick me up at the airport. Even though it was her day off today, I was all the more thankful. Two hours on a train seemed unthinkable right now. Ellis stormed towards me like a crazy person and hugged me enthusiastically.

"How was… Oh, you look awful! Did you catch something? Or was it the flight? I'm sure! Come on, I'll get you back on your feet. Strong coffee and a donut. Let's drive home first. You have to tell me everything," she laughed and linked arms with me. I dozed a little on the way home, and every now and again these songs kept sounding through to me.   (103)

One and a half hours later, we finally got in. All I wanted was to take a bath, drink a glass of wine, and go straight to bed. I assumed that Ellis had different plans. As soon as I came in the door I found a bottle of champagne and flowers on the table. A CD was laying next to the flowers. It was my favourite music, the soundtrack of Lord of the Rings. But why would Ellis give me something like that and trouble herself when I got home? If anything, she'd put down a bottle of whiskey and wait for me to get ready so we could go down to the next pub. Ellis' face showed me that I was right. At the same moment, the doorbell rang. Who would...? I checked quickly and got another shock. It was Mike. He knocked and waved at me, a rose in his hand.

"Hey El, good to see you're back. I... I tried to come pick you up at the airport, but apparently Ellis was faster. Please, El, let me in," he begged. To my dismay, my neighbour just then needed to get through the front door, and just like that he was standing in front of me. Ellis rolled her eyes.

"Thanks, Ellis, for doing my job for me, but it was really not necessary. Can I talk to El for a sec?" He pushed past me into the living room. I really did not have the patience for that.

"Mike, please, I'm dead tired. I need a bath and then   (104) want to go straight to bed. Can't this wait?" I asked him, slightly annoyed. But he made no move to leave.

"Oh, no worries, I'll whisk up something to eat and run the water for you. If you're not too tired after that, we can talk, or maybe not." He winked at me, but I felt nothing but annoyance. He just couldn't accept that I had divorced him and that I had zero interest in him. Of course I knew what he was after. He was trying to get me into bed, but those times were long gone.

"Mike, please. Let's talk some other time. I have a horrible headache and I really can't be around anyone right now," I tried to get rid of him, but Mike played deaf. Ellis saw me between a rock and a hard place and was reliable. In front of the door, she started screeching.

"Ew, oh God, Mike, please, there... There's a giant spider. It is trying to come inside. Please kill it," she screamed and Mike took the bait. He just couldn't help himself. He went to look for it in the hallway.

"Where is it? I can't see any spider," he said and Ellis came closer for a moment.

"There! There it is, right there under the shelf," she   (105) begged and as soon as Mike bent down, my friend slammed the door in his face. "Sorry!" she called from inside.

Mike knocked on the door. "El, what's the big deal? I just want to talk. Come on, El, please open up!" he demanded, but he knew that with Ellis, he was talking to a wall. He also knew that, if he were to keep shouting around, Ellis would have no problem calling the police on him. Behind the door, Ellis was making faces and swearing under her breath. She tried to laugh it off and wanted me to join in, but I was absolutely not feeling it. My head was pounding, the water was running into the tub, and I was fighting back tears. Now she finally looked at me and nearly choked.

"Hey, Mike, please just leave her alone. She really has a horrible headache, must have been the flight. Why don't you get in touch tomorrow morning," she said and immediately came over to me. "Darling, that's not just the headache. Tell me, what happened?" she asked compassionately, all while pouring me a whiskey and pushing me into the bathroom. She helped me get out of my things and light some candles, then she sat down next to me and waited for the bath foam to envelop me. She knew I would talk to her when I was ready. Ten minutes and two glasses of whiskey later, I found my courage. My tears flowed freely and I told her everything from beginning to end. Afterwards, the conversation paused   (106) and Ellis was weeping as well. She was such a crybaby. Either way, I felt a little better already. A small burden had been lifted off my shoulders, and yet Kyran was omnipresent. Two more glasses of whiskey later, this time on Ellis's side, she started to get angry.

"But really, if this guy doesn't even deem it necessary to say goodbye at the airport or send you a text, then... then he doesn't deserve you. Believe me. I mean, there's enough George Clooneys and Brad Pitts out there, fuck those Irish guys."

She was probably right, but it still hurt. And always the question why. My skin was wrinkly and I was properly tired now, so even though I knew I wouldn't sleep, I went off to bed. Ellis had already fallen asleep on the sofa, so I threw a blanket over her. A short glance at my phone. Nothing! Okay, I thought, so that's that. If he hasn't gotten back to me by tonight, then I am done with him. A holiday flirt, nothing more. My head was so empty and wild dreams chased me through the night. The morning didn't look any better. I still had the day off, while Ellis was already gone. I should have gone shopping, but I had no motivation to move. To make matters worse, Mike was already on his way again. Of course he had taken the day off as well. He really wanted to talk to me. The doorbell rang up a storm. If I didn't open the door he   (107) would stand there until the next morning. As soon as I thought that he was gone, a key turned in the lock and the door opened. I was completely baffled when Mike stood before me.

"What??? What in the world? Where did you get that key?!" I thundered. He tried to squirm out of it as usual.

"Oh, I got that for emergencies, you know that! I told you the other day. Don't you remember?" he asked innocently. He always twisted things so they suited him. This truth, too. He knew too well that he hadn't told me anything. I held my hand out for the key, but it disappeared back into his trouser pocket. Holding a basket full of food, he pushed past me into the kitchen and unpacked, then he grabbed pots and pans, completely at home, and started chopping vegetables. I couldn't eat anything. All I really wanted was peace and quiet. I kept glancing at my phone, but the disappointment grew bigger each time. No messages.

"Well, did you meet a new lover?" Mike joked, but I knew that he was pretty jealous. The food was already cooking on the stove.

"Mike, Mike, please, I can't eat one bit. I think the pills and the flight are still weighing me down. Let it be," I said. Mike was pretty disappointed. (108)

"Don't tell me you're lovesick? Heh, some Irish guy, was it, a real man who gave it to you good," he started again. Mike knew he was going too far, but was unable to help himself. I looked at him with disdain.

"I think it is better if you leave now," I said through my teeth and looked past Mike. He came over immediately and grabbed my shoulders, trying to embrace me. My body went stiff and I turned away from him. He had meant to kiss me and now pressed a kiss to my forehead.

"Babe, you know that we belong together. I beg you, give us another chance. I can change, really!" he begged me. He kept hugging me. I couldn't really defend myself, he was too strong and I still had this headache and the feeling of emptiness inside me. Mike was still trying to kiss me, and his grip was growing stronger now. Pressed against the wall, I had nowhere to go, and he pressed his body against mine so that I could feel his erection, but I didn't want to. I made myself as stiff as possible and twisted and turned my head away. Sadly he took this as a challenge to continue. I was starting to get angry.

"Mike!" I tried to talk to him, but he seemed to think I was getting into it and calling his name in arousal. (109)

"Yeah, babe. Come on. I know you want it, too," he said hoarsely and started fumbling with my blouse.

"MIKE!" I screamed into his ear, again and again, until I started yelling, "MIKE, LET ME GO RIGHT NOW!"

Somewhat shocked by my outburst, he was now merely holding my arm, which I immediately wrenched from his grip. "El. Oh, please, El, I am sorry. I... I didn't mean to... But you... You drive me crazy. Can't we... Can't we just put this behind us and start again? Come on, El. I mean, didn't we have good times?" he asked, still out of breath, and I could see his state on his black cloth trousers. Tears sprung to my eyes and I tried my hardest to get out of this mess, so I went over to the door as quickly as I could and opened it.

"I am sorry, Mike, but I just can't. Not like this," I said, then noticed that he was grinning. Had I really said that? He must be thinking that I wanted to try it with him again. But no, no, I didn't want that, not after me and Kyran... Oh God, Kyran. The tears were flowing now and I pushed Mike out the door. "I beg you, Mike, just leave and leave me alone," I begged and just then, my neighbour came in. She looked at us both and shook her head. Of course she couldn't suppress her comments. (110)

"Right, I don't want to call the police again. You alright, sweetheart?" she asked me worriedly. I nodded. She knew how difficult Mike used to be. During one argument, back when we were still a couple, things escalated until Mike smashed a few pieces of furniture, which caused my neighbour to call the police. Since then she had been a thorn in Mike's side anyway. He immediately glared at her.

"Of course she's fine, if you wouldn't stick your nose in her business," he immediately shrieked at her and then muttered, "Old dragon," then he turned back to me, but I had used the opportunity to close the door in his face. Mike knocked and knocked, but he eventually got the message that he wasn't going to get anywhere today. He also couldn't start any problems by attacking my neighbour, as she had quickly disappeared. For a while, I stayed at the door and listened with a racing heart for any noise. Nothing! He had to still be in the hallway. He was also listening at the door. But another ten minutes later he finally gave up. His shoes sounded along the hallway, and shortly after his car door slammed. I rushed to the window and saw him rush off. I really had to change the door locks. That evening I called Ellis, who immediately got upset and started swearing.

"That wanker of a bastard, who does he think he is. He needs a good smack in the mouth. Wow, I could go postal. Darling, are you okay?" she asked all in one breath, which I affirmed. She offered for me to sleep at her place until my locks were changed, but I didn't want that. I thought he had gotten the hint, or so I hoped. Either way, the days went and the nights came. During the day I could distract myself with work. But when the nights approached, I started to wonder and to despair. I had sworn to myself that I would never go on the Ireland webpage again, and especially not log into social networks to look up his band. But I couldn't help myself. I tortured myself. The first entry alone made my tears flow.

"A great gig. The pub was thrilled by Kyran. He has never been as good as today." Alongside it played a tape with a few of his songs. He really was great. When I looked for new photos I found to my delight that there weren't any at the moment. That was good for me, at least I couldn't grieve over them. A list below showed when he was going to play at which location. His list was crammed full. In the background played a slow melody by The Foggy Dew, along with soft background vocals. It was Kyran. One shiver chased the next. In my dreams, Kyran's face haunted me every evening. I was only a husk. Nonetheless I had to manage my everyday affairs somehow. Ellis also noticed the change.   (112)

"Sweetie, are you not feeling well?" she kept asking. But she knew that I wasn't, even though I brushed her off every time. "Come on, forget the guy, he's not worth it if he doesn't even get back to you. Let's go out again some time, think of something else," she tried to bribe me. But I felt like anything but partying. So I crawled back into my shell.

Chapter Eight

Slowly, the weeks passed by, and now I was no longer sitting in front of my computer all day, looking at or listening to future gigs. If only I had! No, I had decided to turn my back on all of it. At least for a while.

The days also got nicer and sunnier, which made Ellis happy. I surprised her with a few nice, extensive walks and visits to ice cream parlours, as well as to pubs or bistros. I still didn't have the necessary ambition to go to evening events. Ellis was pleased. Just like on that day. We were just strolling through the shopping centre, and I indulged myself in an exclusive perfume which smelled amazingly of musk. I loved that scent. After that we passed a Bistro and Ellis urgently needed the loo.

"Oh, El, please, I can't hold it anymore. Let's nip in there a sec, we'll drink a brown ale and then we can leave again. I'll even treat you," she begged and nodded at the eatery. It was a small, cosy bistro with a large glass door and windows, and a few tables with tealights on them had been arranged in front of it. Along the walls stood a few old wooden tables and matching chairs, which were covered in blankets for   (114) people who easily got cold in the evenings. In the background, soft violin music was playing. It sounded Irish,making me hesitate, but Ellis squinted at me so badly that I feared for the worst if we didn't go in.

"All right, all right, but just one beer," I reprimanded her and just like that, Ellis zipped past me, called out to the waitress "I'll get a brown ale," and was not seen again. She quickly ran down the stairs to the toilets and I took a seat on a wooden bench. I didn't really feel like a dark beer, but I didn't know what else to take. The waitress came over with the brown ale and put it down next to me.

"And what can I get you? We have Guinness from the tap today," she said pleasantly and lit the tealight. Before I knew it, I had already nodded my agreement. And when Ellis came back, visibly relieved, her incredulous gaze fell on my glass of Guinness, but she didn't say anything. I just sipped it. The fine, foamy taste bedewed my lips and brought with it an explosion of emotions. No, I didn't want to reminisce. I quickly tried to distract myself by staring at the people that passed us by. But that wasn't a good idea, either. Most people who were around in the evening seemed to be coupled up. Great, I thought and instead stared at the menu as if I was trying to learn it by heart. Ellis saw my face and was just about to (115) get up and go when suddenly, my phone rang. Oh no, I thought, I've heard nothing from Mike all this time, has he relapsed again after all? I didn't even dare to look at the display, and yet there was a curiosity that made the hairs on my neck stand up. It was an unknown number. Ellis rolled her eyes.

"Tell the dosser that if he ever dares to touch you again, I'll give him a thrashing. You just tell him that. Oh, you know what, give that to me!" She snapped her fingers and I was happy to grant her that pleasure. Even if I was a bit embarrassed. Ellis took off with the next ring and growled into the receiver.

"You dirty little piece of shit, if you ever touch her again you can get your tail... what, erm, *how...* I mean... *what...*" she switched between German and English, stuttered and looked quite confused. Then she handed the phone back to me and looked at me.

"What?" I asked right away. "Who was that? Wasn't it Mike?" I asked and got quite the shock. She had just yelled at someone else for no reason, and in my name.

"There was some kind of signal failure. I couldn't understand him properly. He just said something like Sean...   (116)

Mistake… Don't let them… Foolery… And then… His missus and you?" I stared at Ellis. What was that supposed to mean? Goodness gracious, who had that been? Or was Mike playing a prank on us?

"Didn't he say his name? I mean, you said something about a Sean, right?" But Ellis focused on her glass. My face turned as red as a bomb.

"Look, maybe it was a wrong number. It happens. If it was really important, he will call again, believe me," Ellis said and drained her glass in one go. Then she patted my shoulder, paid, and we left. I couldn't believe it. I had to know who that had been. As soon as we were on our way, I couldn't bear it anymore. I had to know who had called me and why. I looked up the number on the internet. It couldn't be, but it really was the Irish country code. My heart nearly stopped, but what had Ellis said, a Sean, why Sean? My fingers flew over the buttons, and before I could help myself I called back the number. It rang and rang, but nothing. Nothing happened. I shot Ellis a desperate look. She seemed really shocked.

"Dear me, that guy really meant something to you. The whole shebang, heartache and all?" she asked again and all I could do was nod with misty eyes. Hanging our heads, we marched into my flat. All I did after that was to hang in front   (117) of my computer and stare at my damn phone. There was neither an update nor a message from Kyran. After about two hours, even Ellis grew tired of me. She muttered something about having no more time and added in a whisper that she had to do something. And she was out the door. My shell was mine alone again and I gave in to the memories. After hours of staring at the computer, even I had to admit defeat. Ellis was right, I had to finally stop thinking about him and forget him. After all, he hadn't gotten in contact with me even once, which showed his character right there. The realisation hit me like a thunderclap. He had merely used me, just like one of his groupies. Well done, Elara, really great. I slammed my laptop shut and downed a glass of wine before sinking into my bed.

Time trickled on, and slowly summer announced its presence. The days grew hotter and the nights shorter. I threw myself into my work until I forgot almost everything else. Next to my job at the supermarket, I now also took on clients as a cleaner. Not that I needed the money, although of course everyone always does, but it was really oblivion I was seeking. It helped for a while, but at night the ghosts came back again. My friend Ellis was also always busy. She acted very secretive and always spoke of our holiday. As if I felt like going away again. No thanks. I had enough of that. I mean, I felt okay at the moment, although I had to say that it   (118) helped that Mike hadn't been in touch since that argument. Had he really given up? Well, I was not about to count my chickens before they were hatched. Either way, Ellis kept pestering me when I would have holiday again so that we could at least go away for a few days. I didn't mean to rain on her parade, but I just didn't want to. The mere thought of a holiday made me start shivering. The memory was still omnipresent.

"Oh, please, Ellis, we've been through this," I complained. Ellis was immediately up in arms.

"Listen to me, I know you had a crappy trip and now you're just moping around like a wet blanket. Seriously, you could have just stayed with Mike then. Goodness gracious. You have to dispose of this baggage once and for all. It's like… like you're a ghost who cannot go into the light because she still has something she needs to do on earth."

I looked at her uncomprehendingly. "What in the world do you mean by that?" I asked, confused. Then Ellis grabbed my shoulders and looked me in the eyes.

"Listen, I know I have made a huge mistake, but I can't stand to see you like this anymore. How you just do your work every day so you can forget. Do you think I haven't noticed how(119) you flinch every time you hear Irish music, or even just hear about Ireland on the telly? Please," she begged me. Goodness gracious, I still had no idea what she was talking about... "Okay," Ellis continued and stared at me stubbornly. "Listen, I know you are going to rip me a new one, but I have to tell you, I did it." She blinked.

My voice broke and I hardly dared to ask her more. "Did what? Ellis!" I warned her. Now she was squirming.

"Fine, I booked us a flight. In June, for four days, to Dublin."

Chapter Nine

That made an impact. My face was already turning red.

"What were you thinking? Oh no, I am not flying. No way." I crossed my arms and pouted like a teenager. But of course I knew Ellis.

"Well, I don't care what you do. I haven't had any holiday yet and believe me, I will fly. With or without you. Oh and you know what, I will even visit a couple of pubs," she grinned. I could do what I wanted. She had won. On the one hand she was right, I had to face my demons and finally know for certain. Also, who was to say that I was flying to Dublin just because of *him*. I hadn't meant to make it this easy for Ellis, but she could see on my face that she had won me over. So once again I got ready for Ireland. It was only one month until then, and I was as nervous as never before. I kept running to the toilet with nervousness, causing Ellis to comment that I ought to take some pills or at least drink a glass of vodka each day. Oh, that was good. A vodka regimen would help for sure. Two days before the trip, I actually did end up drinking half a bottle. Otherwise I never would have made it through the weekend.

We were leaving Monday and had booked a room in one of the hotels right by O'Connell Street until Thursday, so right in the thick of it and only a few minutes away from Temple Bar with all its pubs and pulsing life. Of course I had checked in advance where Kyran would be playing. Sadly I had to find that the page was performing maintenance and would only show the dates on short notice. Great, I thought, but after all I wasn't flying for him. Or so I hoped. Before we left, Ellis glanced into my suitcase and shook her head in pity.

"Good grief, we are not doing a sightseeing trip for tourists. Are you sure you want to bring this?" she asked distrustfully and looked into my travelbag with disgust. I thought I had packed everything for a practical day: Jeans, sweater, two shirts, a trenchcoat and my bootees.

"Why? I don't know. It's all practical. After all we will be running around a lot. And the weather is just typically Irish," I defended myself. Ellis was already rummaging in my wardrobe.

"Yeah, fine for Ireland, but you forget where we are going. It's *the* party street par excellence. If you need to, keep the jeans, but you need to add something with pep, and something sexy for the evenings. So... Hmmm, here... Just the thing." (122)

She held up a black mini dress with lace trim and, well, let's call it figure hugging. Her grin was ear-splitting. "Wear this and men will fall at your feet," she laughed. Goodness, I wasn't going just to pull someone, but internally I already saw myself stand in front of Kyran. No, no, I had to stop with that. Ellis also packed a couple of casual blouses in my bag: a black one, slightly translucent, but without showing too much, as well as a wide, white one. I was allowed to take my bootees, but a few pumps would come along as well. Topped off with a short blazer and my black leather jacket. Fine, so be it.

In the early morning we got on our way and took the train to the airport. On the train I allowed myself a piccolo to be able to approach everything relaxedly. One turned into two and all that on an empty stomach, since I could never eat before trips because of my nervousness.

Once we got to the airport, we still had an hour's time. Ellis took the time to fill her stomach, while mine rewarded me with acid regurgitation. A sip of cola and a tablet against nausea, done and dusted. Although the things sadly showed their side effects, especially in connection with the alcohol I'd had earlier. I ran through the terminal like a junkie hippie. Once on the plane, tiredness overcame me and I dozed the whole ninety minutes until we landed in Dublin. The trip continued immediately via bus shuttle, which had been sent by the (123) hotel. We drove for nearly ten miles before the bus stopped on O'Connell Street, right opposite our hotel. It was a simple, but old hotel and super snug. The people there greeted us affectionately and we received our keys. As soon as we got into the room, Ellis rushed to the window.

"Wow, look at that, we can see directly down to the main street. And back there is the sea, but really tiny," she laughed and threw herself on one of the single beds. All in all the room was kept simple. Two single beds with red duvet covers, next to them two small chests of drawers, a wardrobe, a small table with chairs, and on one wall a flat screen TV. Right next door was a small bathroom with a shower.

"Oh, come on, El, let's eat a bite and then go shopping," Ellis laughed and tossed her clothes on the bed. Then she disappeared into the bathroom and emerged ten minutes later, fresh as the morning dew. It was no use protesting. I grabbed my things as well, cleaned myself up and put my hair up at the sides. Despite being in the inner city, a strong wind was blowing here. I put on my pre-ripped jeans, which were skin-tight without being restricting, together with a blouse and a cardigan over the top, and of course my bootees. I felt good. By now, I was also getting a little peckish. Time to see what the city had to offer.

We linked arms and marched merrily past the reception. A young man was standing there, he had to be an Englishman judging by the accent when he called after us.

"Hey, have a great time. Wow!" he whistled and it really made my day, even though I felt somewhat intimidated when I saw all the women and girls who passed us by. Everyone looked really great, just natural, but whatever, I thought. We are who we are.

We spent all day ambling through Dublin. We began with the snack booths, where we stopped at a shop selling fish 'n' chips with vinegar as well as deep-fried mars bars, delicious. Then we sauntered over to Trinity College and drank a coffee to go, with which we sat down on the steps to the college, where other people were already sitting. Everyone was talking over one another. At times we could hear an Irish accent, then again a typically British one, but also Italian, Turkish, and the one or other German. This city was truly alive. Once evening approached, we started another walk towards Penny Bridge, which was crossing the river Liffey. Again we sat, holding an ice cream cone, and enjoyed the breeze wafting over from the river. My heart started racing. This was where I had sat with Kyran. Memories awoke and slowly I began to panic.   (125)

"Wow, what's going on?" Ellis asked worriedly. "Is it the journey? Hmm, maybe it's all been a bit too much?" she asked again, but I just shook my head. Now the penny dropped. "Oh, you mean… You and that guy. I get it. Okay then, come on." She grinned and pulled me up by the hand. She moved in the direction of the hotel.

"Oh Ellis, I am so sorry, but I can't help it. Please don't be mad," I moaned, but Ellis merely laughed.

"Silly, I just need the loo pretty desperately," she grinned and crossed her legs a little. Now I was laughing as well and we walked back to the hotel. We were planning to go back to Temple Bar in two hours to have a Guinness. I was already thinking of an excuse why I couldn't go.

"Umm, listen, I think I am getting a stomach bug or something. Maybe we shouldn't do everything at once today," I tried. As soon as I said it, a bottle with drops came flying towards me.

"No chickening out. After all, we're only here for four days and one of them is basically over. I want to experience all I can. Take twenty and you'll be good as new," she instructed and pointed at the bottle. I obeyed and waited. Really, ten minutes later my stomach no longer felt quite so wobbly.   (126)

Nonetheless I was feeling a bit ill. Fear emerged. Ellis came out of the bathroom and looked styled as never before. Her hair was sticking out as if she had been walking through a storm, but she quickly combed them and they laid perfectly again. She was wearing a mini skirt, a blouse with flower print, and boots. She threw on a poncho and pulled a bottle of prosecco out of her suitcase. No idea where she got that, since liquids were not permitted in hand luggage. I had probably still been half asleep when she got the bottle at the airport. Either way we clinked glasses while I got changed. Ellis insisted on me wearing the little black number. At first I didn't want to, I just wasn't feeling it. But after the second glass I loosened up a little. Ellis was right, I didn't look half bad. So I grabbed my leather jacket and we moved out.

Life here at Temple Bar was at its fullest this time of year. Teens, students, tourists and natives mingled here. I was surprised to see a few older people as well. But exactly that was special about this place. It was possible to party and to relax. Even if it was the middle of the week. One pub followed the next, mixed with some snack shacks. Everywhere I looked, young people were standing in the streets chatting and smoking. Some were clearly already more than tipsy, but everyone stayed friendly. The first pub we headed for was right around the corner. It was crammed full. There was (127) no live band yet, or alternatively we had to try harder to find one. We found two places at a corner table and Ellis got us a Guinness and a glass of Paddy's, an Irish whiskey. She went straight for the hard stuff. I didn't mind; the sooner I was tipsy, the sooner I could go back to the hotel.

The people around us chatted and laughed, and it was fascinating to see what they were all like. I immediately felt better with the first sip of whiskey, which ran down my throat with a slight burning sensation. The evening stretched out and we toured from one pub to the next. Ellis kept grabbing men that were either gay or practically still in diapers. Fine, the occasional one of them was all right. By the end, we were running around with three other people, a couple and some guy who was a backpack tourist putting up camp in the city. He was driving around Ireland with the goal to ultimately visit every country. Ellis was visibly attracted to him. Long hair and sadly also slightly greasy, shirt and jeans waistcoat which had seen better days, ripped jeans and boots with holes. He kept his guitar continually in his hands, trying to jingle. Fine, he wasn't all that bad. I don't know, he just looked as if he was permanently high or at least a complete eco freak. Not that I minded that, but he kept trying to lure us in in this snotty way, like "Hey, man," and "Hey dude, that's rad," and that after every second word. No idea what my friend saw in him. (128)

Either way, the evening got later and later. Most pubs now had live bands playing. We also went from pub to pub. In what felt like the twelfth pub we went in as well. Another Guinness. The band was just taking a break and people were milling around outside to smoke or just get some fresh air. The couple had left us in the meantime, we lost them somewhere between pubs five and nine. Of course David, the freak, stayed with us, which greatly pleased Ellis. They were stuck at a table and I had to relieve myself after the Guinness. It wasn't that easy. Everyone was in the way and ran to the toilets at the same time. It was no use, I queued. Ten minutes later, it was finally my turn. All at once, the room emptied. What... But I hadn't even gone yet. Idiot me. Now I finally realised that the stage was filling again and the pre-band was playing. I was just washing my hands, using my perfume to refresh the room. I nearly dropped the flask. The band was playing The Foggy Dew, a faster version, and yet so familiar. Was I hearing things? Could that really be Kyran's voice? My knees were shaking and I quickly gave myself a once-over in the mirror. A flick of the wrist here, a curl falling into my forehead there, and lots of perfume. Goodness gracious, Elara, what are you doing? You were going to forget about him. But my feet were not obeying me. They did what they wanted and I squeezed my way through to the front of the room. To the band. Internally, I was praying that it wasn't Kyran. It seemed   (129) like my prayers were answered. It was not his band. Relieved, but with a racing heart, I pushed my way back to Ellis and David. I was so lost in my thoughts that I hardly noticed when a man bashed into me.

"Oh, sorry," I muttered.

The man merely growled back. "No worries." But then he added a hissed "Typical jaffy tourists," which I just about still heard. I turned around to call him out on his behaviour. After all, I had had a few pints of Guinness, and they were starting to affect me. I was a bit talkative. When I went to confront him, I turned too fast and bashed into a Chinese exchange student who was carrying a beer. He spilled it and it landed on the rude guy. Now he was especially angry.

"Great, now I can perform in a puddle of beer and stink like hell. Awesome. You... you... YOU?" he shouted and my mood fell even further. Kyran himself was standing in front of me. I didn't know if I should laugh or cry, or if I should throw my arms around his neck or run away. I stared at him with my mouth open. "What are you doing here?" he asked me and I tried to reply.

"I, umm, I am spending a few days of holiday. You... You're performing today?" I asked back. Stupid question. He was about to answer, but his oh so great pal Dyllon was already calling him from the stage. He waved at him and then glanced back at me one more time.

"Will you still be here later?" he asked and I nodded. Whatever, the day couldn't get worse. In a bad mood I returned to Ellis and David, who were so caught up in their conversation that they hadn't even noticed I was gone. I sipped at my drink and as soon as I heard Kyran's voice I could have burst into tears. Three songs later I couldn't bear it anymore and went outside. Only now Ellis noticed something and stomped after me.

"Hey sweetheart, what's up?" she giggled, but I shook my head and simply said that I was feeling a bit dizzy and just needed some air. I would be fine soon and come back in. Ellis left and joined back up with David. Four more songs and the band stopped. Dyllon thanked the audience, also in the name of Kyran. Ellis's glass rang against the table and she stared at me.

"THAT... That's HIM?" she spat. I just nodded. As soon as he was off the stage, Dyllon walked past us and grinned at me.

Kyran also came back to me, but he just shook my hand and muttered dejectedly. "Maybe we'll meet again later. Have fun," he just said dryly and exchanged a look with his pal.   (131)

I turned red and was at a loss for words. The band stepped away a bit and I heard Ellis fuss.

"Goodness gracious, did I miss something? This... This tit, excuse my French, is the reason for your months of bad mood. Now we're here and he treats you like you're invisible? That's unbelievable. That guy is a few short of a full set." She was beside herself and wanted to run straight after him, but I just about managed to hold her back.

"Ellis, leave it. There's no point. It's over," I sighed. Sadly, tears were forming in my eyes, but Ellis didn't really notice. Her alcohol levels had risen steadily throughout the last pubs.

"But... But he... He can't just..." she stammered and her fury rose again, but mister "hey-dude-that's-rad" just eladetly took her in his arms and started dancing through the pub with her.

"Ellis, I am going back to the hotel. I've had enough for today," I said and lowered my head. Just as Kyran was sitting back down by the bar. I actually meant to go to him, but at the same moment, Dyllon appeared with the rest of the band. They were towing a young woman along, perhaps in her mid twenties, with long brown hair and a typically Irish face. When she saw Kyran, she approached him enthusiastically and hugged him passionately. He took her in his arms and kissed her. That was too much for me. I finally had enough and left.   (132)

Ellis waved after me and called out, "Don't wait up, it could get late," and grinned at David. But she did look past me and saw where I had been looking. Thankfully our hotel wasn't far from Temple Bar. It only took me a few minutes to get there. Most people were still out and about, which was understandable. For this one evening, the weather was amazing. It was dry, not too cool, but also not too hot. But they beauty stayed hidden from me and my head started pounding. A nice bath would be great now, I thought, but the hotel didn't have a bathtub. So all I wanted was to hide my head under a pillow and lose myself in my sadness. If Ellis hadn't been there with me, I would have gone to the airport the next day and taken the first plane home. What nonsense had possessed me, anyway? Why on earth hadn't I just gone to the north sea or stayed at home in the first place? I felt god-awful. Still in my evening outfit, I threw myself on the bed and allowed my tears to flow freely. The sounds of the night still drifted in from outside. Mingling voices and car sounds were accompanied with live music, which was slowly lulling me to sleep. My sleep was a gruelling doze, which was interrupted by an unbearable ringing noise. I woke up and had to orientate myself for a second. The room was dark and only a slim sliver of light came in from the street. My hand searched for the night light. I turned it on, and I really didn't want to look at my   (133) phone display, but the ringing didn't stop. Just turn it off, I thought and was about to do the same when I saw that it was Ellis's number. Was she so drunk now that she couldn't even find her David anymore? Fine, just to put an end to it.

"What is it, Ellis?" I asked, slightly annoyed. While my friend was trying to answer, I could hear a loud babble of voices in the background.

"El, sweetheart, can you please, please come get me. I... I had a horrible fight with David and he just up and left. That idiot. Please, he didn't pay his tab and I really don't have enough on me. I swear you'll get it back right away, but these guys are not joking around. El, please. El, can you hear me?"

I just nodded until I noticed what I was doing. "Oh. Yes, of course. Where are you?" I asked, hoping she wasn't still in the bar Kyran had been playing in. But she was. What was I to do? Okay, I thought to myself.

"All right, listen, I'll come to the door and you go there, then I give you the money and we can leave," I said, sensing victory.

"Okay, no problem," Ellis simply said and hung up. Great, now I had to go out again despite my rotten mood. A bit of powder on my face so I didn't look quite as puffy from crying,   (134) on with my boots and leather jacket, and off I went again. At the reception, only the night light was burning, and loud music was still coming through the wall from the joined pub. It was now pretty empty on the street as well. Most people had gone home or were scattered around some bars and pubs. The pub Ellis was still in had gone quieter as well. Most bands had stopped playing and all that could be heard was active conversation noise. The pub was still crammed. I waited and waited in front of the entrance. No Ellis. This couldn't be happening. Had she been so drunk that she had just made a break for it? I waited a few more minutes before I had enough and went back inside. Immediately, I was assaulted by the smell of old wood, mixed with beer and whiskey as well as sweat. It wasn't displeasing, I found. First, I went to the table Ellis had been at last, but she wasn't there. Then I went to the toilets and made sure she wasn't hanging over one of the bowls. No Ellis here, either. Damn, where could she be? The pub wasn't too big, so I walked around some more. Something made me seek out the bar. I couldn't say what, but an inner instinct told me I needed to be there. My heart raced and just like that, I saw him sit at the bar. Kyran! He was bent over. A glass of whiskey and a pint of Guinness were standing in front of him. I quarrelled with myself over whether I should go to him or turn around. Suddenly, someone pushed me from behind and steered me unerringly towards Kyran.   (135)

"What... Hey, no... What are you doing?" I panted. My head spun around and I saw Ellis and David together, who grinned at me. Oh no, count me out. With all my might, I fought back against the two. But with two against one, I didn't stand a chance. They pushed me ever further along.

"Ellis, for heaven's sake, what are you doing? Please stop this," I begged her. I looked around for help, but apparently everyone around us thought we were joking around. I even thought I could see Sean in the middle of the crowd. He grinned and laughed and waved at me. That was the limit! And now I bashed into Kyran. He didn't even look up, but merely muttered something under his breath. Ellis pushed me right into the bar.

"Talk to him!" she ordered.

I shook my head. "No, I... I just can't. Please, Ellis, if you planned all this, then I believe we have nothing left to say to each other." I really meant it. What did she think she was doing? And most importantly, why? Everything was crystal clear after all. And now Kyran finally saw me. His eyes were shining and yes, he was a little tipsy.
"Oh, the pretty Elara," he sing-sang. What a wonderful start.

"Well, we meet again," I said dryly and cursed Ellis. She had already dashed off with Hey-Cool-Dude-David. What could I do except take the offensive. Admittedly I wasn't as sober as I would have liked either, but honestly, whatever. I ordered a Guinness and a glass of Paddy's whiskey. Then I demonstratively sat down next to him.

"Hey," I said and he just nodded. Great. I sipped my beer and an awkward silence fell. We sat next to each other like strangers. What was I supposed to say to him, I thought. I quickly downed my glass of whiskey. After a few minutes, I had enough. I finally wanted to clear the air. As soon as I opened my mouth, someone interrupted me again. Dyllon. He came straight to me and squeezed between me and Kyran.

"Oh, wow, if it isn't the heartbreaker," he sang and grinned at me.

"Hey, what have I ever done to you?" I asked him bluntly and glared at him. He pulled me to the side with a gentle, but determined grip.

"Listen, you may have been a nice change of pace for him, but certainly nothing serious. He has no use for that kind of thing. It distracts him too much. I saw it. He wasn't himself anymore. Leave it be and put it down as a little adventure," he said, all business. Then he pushed me somewhat rudely (137) away from the bar and added, "Go back to your husband. Maybe he hasn't found out about your affair yet," he warded me off. I was so confused that at first, I didn't understand what he was saying, but then I saw Sean again. He was gesturing with his arms and kept pointing at me and at Kyran.

I kept mulling it over until the penny dropped. "Wait a second," I called out. "What do you mean, my husband?" I asked Dyllon sharply, and now I was the one pulling him rudely aside.

"Listen, babe. When you went home, I went through your online profiles, and what do you know, every single one said you were happily married to Mike." My mouth fell open and I turned red. That was the last straw. I pushed Dyllon aside and screamed at Kyran.

"That's why you didn't say anything, why you never called. Because of MIKE?!" I was all but screaming and ran my hands through my hair. Kyran looked at me. "MIKE, that nutter, is my ex husband, but you already know about him. He just can't accept that we are divorced and keeps embarrassing me wherever he can. If you found that on the internet then maybe you should have kept reading. My real profile has more posts and photos than my fake profile, which was probably hacked by Mike. He is a hopeless nutter. (138)

But what am I saying," I whinged, upset. Dyllon just laughed and tried to wave it off as a joke.

"Oh, believe me, it's better this way. Kyran is better off without you," he just said and downed a whiskey.

"Yeah, since he apparently already has a girlfriend," I said and looked at Kyran. Was Dyllon hesitating before he grinned?

"You know it, sweetheart, so forget about him, go back to Good Old Germany, and all is well," he laughed. Ellis, who had watched everything from a corner, now stormed over to Dyllon.

"Right, I've had it up to here. Elara has been upset by this whole thing far more deeply than you think. THAT guy there is the dosser after all, and shitbag Mike is a dosser, too. He lies as the day is long. If someone has messed up, it's him," she pointed at Kyran. Now Sean was getting involved as well. He swiftly pulled me aside.

"I am sorry, but I've tried to call you," he said quietly and pulled me further into a corner.
"You called me?" I repeated and Sean nodded.
"You see, when you were gone Kyran wasn't doing well. I mean, I may just be the driver, but I hear a lot. Anyway, the evening you went home I noticed how Dyllon kept   (139)

paying for Kyran's drinks until the man could hardly stand. Of course he missed the flight the next day. But that is not all, Dyllon also started talking trash. He told Kyran things, like that you were snogging other Irish guys as well, and when he saw some old profiles he just went ahead and called up this Mike. He found one or two old pictures and rubbed them in Kyran's face. Said you were still with your ex. It completely derailed Kyran, and now, when he saw you here again, it was easy to show him another profile which is allegedly a current one. I mean, I don't know, but is it really true? About you and your ex, or is it still your husband?" he asked, looking insecure.

My head was spinning. A sea of lies and deceit. Oh, Mike was going to pay for this. But first it was Dyllon's turn. I glared at him. Was he guessing something? He pressed really close to Kyran, and before I knew it, I was pushed aside by the rest of the band. Dyllon whispered something in the lead singer's ear and he got up. Kyran glanced at me, then he shrugged and linked arms with Dyllon. Both marched, or in Kyran's case wobbled, out of the pub and stopped a taxi. My head was spinning and I really needed to get out. With misty eyes I ran down the street, along the Liffey, to the end of the O'Connell Bridge. There I stopped for a moment to take a breath and breathe in the air. My tears were running like a river now. That was it for me, I decided. Tomorrow, I would take the next (140) plane and fly home. To make matters worse, my phone was vibrating again and I made the mistake to risk a glance. Of course, Dyllon had been nice enough to send me a picture of Kyran arm in arm with the brunette. Below that he had written, with a smiley, "Sorry, but don't take it too hard. It wasn't meant to be." I turned my phone off completely. I had enough. One more time I inhaled the air, and then went back to the hotel. I was completely lost in thought and really wasn't thinking of Ellis anymore. Whatever, when she came home to the hotel, she would just have to knock.

Chapter Ten

Downstairs in the in-house pub I could still hear a babble of voices, and the occasional figure was traipsing around outside the door. A young man staggered towards me and started talking to me. I could not understand a word. Firstly because he was slurring extremely, and secondly because because he was speaking Irish. I quickly squeezed past him and scurried into the hotel entrance. I did manage to take a short glance into the pub. Some guests were still hanging around the bar, and two lonely couples were sitting at the tables. One person quickly flitted across the dancefloor in the direction of the toilets. I had to be seeing things. From behind, the guy looked exactly like Mike. That couldn't be, I told myself. On the other hand, I would absolutely trust Mike to do something like that. Should I risk another look? But what if it was really Mike? I believed myself capable of tearing apart the whole pub. Instead, I rather went to bed, hoping to catch some sleep. Which apparently was not meant to be. I tossed and turned. Every few minutes, I stared at the clock. Only one hour had passed since I had laid down. A few people were still bellowing outside the hotel and now started to sing Irish songs. No trace of Ellis. I went into the bathroom and doused my face with cold water. My reflection looked terrible. (142)

Puffy eyes and red cheeks. At the same time, my stomach felt queasy and my head was pounding. I took some drops and a pill. Then I went back to bed and waited for everything to start working. Car headlights threw long and slightly scary shadows on the walls, accompanied by sounds from one of the neighbouring rooms that were definitely coming from two couples making love. I rolled onto my side pulled the blanket over my head. Thankfully, this allowed me to get a little rest.

I woke up with the first sunshine. The room was still just as empty. My head was throbbing. Where was Ellis? I was starting to get worried. Nonetheless, I wanted to stick to my plan. I freshened up, got dressed, and heaved my suitcase on the bed to pack it. As soon as I was done with that, I decided to go to the hotel restaurant to drink a strong coffee. Of course I wasn't planning to just leave without a word. After all, Ellis had to know what was going on. Before I entered the restaurant I stopped at the reception desk and asked for messages. Nothing! Not from Ellis and also not from Ky… Oh come on, I scolded myself. Why should he of all people leave a message here? I really needed a coffee. The restaurant was not too busy yet. A few younger people were scattered around the tables, and on two of them sat older couples who were chatting amicably. I took a seat in the hindmost corner. Both a toast with jam and some coffee got stuck in my throat. (143)

I took a last glance around the room and was just about to get up when a young man entered the room. At first I barely noticed him, but when I looked a second time, my heart nearly stopped. Over by the coffee machine really was Mike. This could only be a nightmare. I rubbed my eyes and looked again. Phew, it had been a nightmare. My breath was coming more slowly already. I just had to go crazy in this place, I thought and laughed to myself. Then I looked up and choked on my laughter. A young man with a cup of coffee in his hand was standing in front of me, grinning sweet as pie.

"Before you lose it, yes, I went after you, but only because I had this weird feeling I would lose you here. I am sorry. May I sit down?" Before I could reply, Mike grabbed a chair and sat down next to me. He kept stirring his coffee. I stared at him with my mouth open. My head and brain were trying to find the right words. But all they found were a "Why?" and a dark glare. Internally, I was about to explode. He was already reaching for my hand, which I quickly pulled away.

"Listen, I didn't mean to come after you, but when this strange guy texted me and said that this man is not good for you, I just had to come. Please, El, believe me, I didn't mean to bother you." Mike looked deep into my eyes, but my head was growing hot and I was as shaky as if I was on a rollercoaster. I needed to get out of here before I could make a scene   (144) and use the dishes as a weapon. Mike tried to stop me, but I unmistakably signalled him with my finger that he needed to be quiet and went out for air. Outside I crossed the street and walked towards the bridge railing that separated me from the Liffey. I leaned over it to suck in the air, which was laden with salt. As soon as I had arrived, Mike was standing behind me again.

"El, please, say something?" he begged me. When I turned around, I looked at him with so much hatred in my eyes that even he had to take a few steps back.

"What in the world made you come here? And what guy, anyway? What were you thinking?" I thundered. Mike started to squirm. He dared to come a few steps closer again and tried to grab my shoulders, but I held up my hands in defense. "Don't touch me!" I hissed.

Mike came closer again and tried to talk to me very calmly and tenderly. "El, babe, I know you are angry, but you don't deserve a guy like that. Believe me, he was just messing with you. I mean, here, look, all the pictures with the gorgeous, I apologise, with the girl here. I'm just saying, please, it's not your fault. Forget him! Maybe you can give us another chance, here and now," he begged and was about to   (145) take a knee. Was he going to propose to me?! No, no, no, he wasn't allowed to do that. No, and I didn't want to. No way.

"MIKE!" I screamed at him. "Damn it, get up. What do you mean by the guy and the girl?" I hissed. My ex pulled out his phone and tapped it nervously, while gesturing with the other hand for me to stay here. After a few seconds, he found what he had been looking for and gave me his phone. He had opened a social network and presented to me a few photos of Kyran with that brunette. I had meant to look at the pictures more closely, but Mike immediately ripped the phone from my hands again.

"I beg you, El, don't torture yourself with this. What I want to say is that this guy was playing a game with you. Please understand that. I mean, what other proof do you need?" He looked at me questioningly and imploringly at the same time. On the one hand, I wanted to believe him. After all, I had seen Kyran and that woman myself, how she hugged and kissed him. What else did I need? Nonetheless, something bothered me. Perhaps it was just that Mike was here.

"Say, how did you even know that I was here?" I asked him and Mike's hopes grew again.

"Well, from you yourself. Alright, actually through Ellis. She was posting-happy and flagged your location. After that, it was easy to find you," he grinned.

"You mean you have been watching me the entire time? You don't say you got a room in the same hotel?" I bristled. Mike nodded only imperceptibly, and when he saw that I was about to go off again, he quickly raised his hands to deflect.

"Yes, I have a room in your hotel, but I swear I didn't follow you all day. I only got here yesterday. And well, I couldn't find you then, so I had a look around by myself. I mean, what do you see in this city? It's anything but pretty, I am sure there are nicer areas. Admit it, Ellis probably convinced you to come here, or maybe just this guy?" he taunted me again. I looked down at the Liffey and watched the sun's reflection in it.

"Of course you don't understand that. There is nothing to understand, after all. You and I have simply always had different views. Don't you understand? We have always been too different. For you, the only important viewpoint is your own, you never allowed for anyone else's. That's why we didn't get along in the long run." Was I really trying to talk to him in a civilised manner? I was probably only kindling the fire again. Speaking of Ellis, where was she anyway? I looked around, which Mike noticed right away.   (147)

"You're not looking for him?" he asked immediately and tried to grab my arm again. I fended him off.

"Goodness gracious, Mike, I meant Ellis!" I snapped at him. He looked at me sheepishly, but with an air of relief.

"Maybe she is back in your room. Let's look there." That was the first reasonable thing I had heard him say. I nodded curtly and walked slowly across the street, approaching the hotel. Mike followed me like a puppy. Now and again he tried to grab my hands, but I crossed them in front of my chest and stubbornly kept walking. In the hotel, I rushed up the stairs so that Mike could hardly keep up. Once we had reached our room, I unlocked it.

"Ellis? Ellis, are you there?" I yelled into it. Now, sure, there weren't many places to look. She could either be in the room or in the bath, but that was empty, too. Goodness gracious, where was she fooling about?

"And?" Mike asked behind me and I startled. I hadn't expected for him to follow me in. I shook my head.

"Hm, not really large for two," Mike said and was now standing in the room. Then he walked over to the window and   (148) looked out. Of course all he saw was the street. "And that's what you pay so much for? I wouldn't have, but it's your decision. So, what's up next?" he asked and slouched down on the bed as if it was the most normal thing in the world. He grinned smugly and his top shirt buttons were suddenly open. He lightly patted the bed next to him. He can't be serious, I thought. Sure, I must have once seen something in him. He was tall, had grey-blue eyes, ash-blond hair and a muscular body. When I had still been with him, I had been only too aware what attraction he had on women. Admittedly, I had been a little proud to show myself with him. But sadly, the years went by and I got to feel intimately what it was like to be married to this man. His true character emerged only through the years. On the outside, he continued to played the loving husband, but when he was alone with his friends, the devil came out to play. He trash talked me behind my back and flirted with everything that was wearing a skirt. Up to the point when I caught him asking out a young woman and telling her he was a free man. In general, we didn't get along so well anymore. He kept trying to regain control of my life and stuck his nose into everything. Well, we all knew the end of it.

"Mike, please get up!" I told him, but he kept patting the duvet. What was he trying to play at here? "Mike, I'm serious. Stop it and get up. I have to find Ellis. And also, I want to get   (149) out of here. My plane leaves at four," I explained. That was a mistake. Mike grinned almost triumphantly. He got up and came really close to me.

"I had wondered why your suitcase is already or still packed. I am happy to take you to the airport and we can go home together," he purred and his hands went around my waist. He pressed me close and his lips found my throat. For a split second, I was about to resist. But I knew that I couldn't. My thoughts were not free. Not free from Mike and especially not from Kyran.

"Mike, please stop and let me go!" I scolded him and tried to get out of his grip. But once again he didn't get it and strengthened his hold of me even more. He kept trying to kiss me and was getting more demanding. Here, I wouldn't be lucky enough to be able to count on my neighbours. I also didn't want to start screaming, that would be too embarrassing. Mike kept trying to push me towards the bed. It wasn't difficult. The room was pretty small, but after all we had wanted to sleep here, not live here. But now it was becoming a trap for me. Mike was stronger and I could already feel the edge of the bed. I didn't want to fall, but it was too late. The edge made me stumble. I was now laying on the bed and
(150)

felt Mike above me, who kept kissing my neck. His breath came faster and faster, and his voice was getting hoarse.

"Oh, El, I missed you so much," he breathed and fumbled with his shirt. Before I knew it, his shirt flew next to the bed and he lay over me topless. His hands were still holding mine while his mouth wandered lower. He kissed my female curves through my sweater and I could definitely feel his erection. A shiver ran down my body, but I knew that even if I slept with him now, nothing would change for me. Mike on the other hand would get his hopes up for nothing, and when I then tried to break it off with him, it would only end in more endless discussions and insults. As well as I could, I tried to squirm free. But his heavy body on mine was too strong for me.

"Mike. Mike! Please stop. There's no point. It's not going to get you anywhere. Mike, please!" I tried to plead with him, but he was playing deaf. His thighs were grinding against my leg in a slow rhythm. Fine, as long as he didn't touch me anywhere I was okay with that. But Mike had other plans. He wanted what he wanted. In the spur of the moment, he was now sitting on top of me. With one hand, he was holding my hands over my head like a vice. I had no idea that one person could have this much strength. I had bad forebodings.

"Mike! Please let me go. You know there is no point. What is this supposed to change? Please, Mike, don't do   (151) anything you will regret," I pleaded shakily. He appeared to me as if intoxicated. My hands in his grip, he had his other one fumbling with my trousers. I tried to make myself as stiff as possible, but it was no use. His fingers slipped into my trousers and his lips pressed hard and demanding against mine. His tongue kept pushing against my resisting lips. I bit him, which was another mistake. His eyes were now sparking madly. I knew I shouldn't have bit him. He looked at me, grinning like a madman. His hand gripped mine even harder, and the other ripped so hard on my zipper that it broke. Then he forcefully turned me around, so that my face was now against the sheet. Now I couldn't fight back at all. My hands were free, but I couldn't defend myself. I struggled to get free with hands and feet, but Mike was now sitting on my legs and ripping on my trousers. Suddenly, I felt something pointy cutting slightly into my leg.

"Mike? Mike, what are you doing?" I yelled in panic. From the corner of my eye, I could see something flash in the light. Of course, I remembered. He always had a small pocket knife on him. But that couldn't be real. Would he really do something like this? His mouth kept kissing my back more passionately and kept wandering down to my hips. I tried to kick my legs, but he was still sitting on me. How should I ever get out of here? There was no use in talking, he was as if   (152) intoxicated. And I couldn't scream either, since I was laying belly-down on the blanket and Mike was nearly strangling me with his weight. I heard his aroused panting and heard how buttons were opened and he nestled with a zipper. Oh goodness gracious, surely he wouldn't just rape me here and now, and yet that was how it seemed all of a sudden.

"MIKE. I beg you. Don't do anything you will regret. Stop. What do you think you are doing? Mike, please. It's no use, this won't bring us back together either. You are just making it worse. MIKE!" I pleaded. But he merely laughed hoarsely.

"Babe, believe me. When I am done with you, you will beg me to come back. We simply belong together, you know that." He nestled at my trousers again to get them off me. Through his thin cotton trousers, I could feel his manhood. He lay down on top of me and tried to spread my legs with his. I fought him as much as I could, but I was so afraid that I couldn't manage it. Tears were now running down my face and I was shaking.

"Please don't do this!" I pleaded, but Mike kept trying to get my trousers down somehow. He had pulled them down far enough that my slip was showing. Mike considered himself close to the goal and moaned out loud.

"Oh, El, you are so hot. You have no idea how much I   (153) missed you. We are simply meant for each other," he breathed. When he was just about to reach the goal of his lust, the door was slammed open and Ellis stormed in. Completely stumped, she stopped dead in the door. She held her hands to her mouth to stop a scream.

"I, oh, I didn't know that Mike, that… you and him. Okay, oops, I can see that I am in the way. But actually - oh nevermind," she stammered, sounding shocked.

Mike panted at her. "Could you just give us a minute. Would you be so kind and leave us alone. Please!" he said sarcastically. Embarrassed, Ellis quickly looked to the side and was about to get back out, while Mike kissed my back like a drunk and his loins kept moving rhythmically. He hadn't reached his goal yet, but it wasn't missing much. Before Ellis had reached the door, I whimpered softly and tried to get her attention. I would have loved to scream at her to do something, but something pointy was cutting into my side. One of Mike's hands was still holding the knife, and it was poking dangerously close to my ribs. What should I do? Think, Elara, I told myself. Then I realised.

"Ellis, sweetheart, it's fine, Mike and I are back together. We… We just couldn't wait. Tell Dyllon I am sorry. Tell   (154) him that, please!" I wheezed as well I could. I really hoped Ellis would get it. But she just shook her head.

"But El, you... I mean. And anyway, Dyllon?" she asked uncomprehendingly. I nodded as much as possible, and Mike was now getting really angry.

"Get out!" he screamed at Ellis, and his knife was now stabbing into my ribs, making me scream. But I had to press my mouth against the blanket, so that it looked as if I was completely aroused. Ellis grabbed the door handle and was just about able to look at me, which I found terribly embarrassing.

"Please tell Dyllon! Promise me!" I begged, and now Mike had enough. He stormed towards Ellis and pushed her to the door. Then he shoved her out with force, and the door locked. For a short moment, I could breathe and tried to get up, but Mike was faster back by my side. He grabbed my wrist and twisted it so that I fell to my knees. He picked me up and tossed me on the bed. What should I do? I tried to sit up, but Mike pulled his knife again and held it in front of my face.

"Mike, I beg you. You don't want to do this. You wouldn't hurt me," my voice shook. But Mike grinned.   (155)

"What do you think?" he asked and bent over me. He tried to forcibly kiss my mouth. But I twisted away each time. Again I felt a prick, this time harder than before. I also felt something wet and warm on my stomach. Now Mike was capable of anything. He showed me the knife again.

"If you don't do what I say, then believe me, this will get ugly. So please pretend at least for a few minutes that you are still my wife. If I want to kiss you, I want you to go along with it, and when I sleep with you I want to hear you. Understood!" he hissed. I did not recognise this Mike, and he scared me terribly, while his knife kept leaving small cuts on my body. Again Mike's tongue stabbed into my mouth, and I reluctantly let it happen. Mike moaned again and nestled with my waistband. He kept trying to pull down my trousers bit by bit. After lots and lots of pushing and pulling he managed to uncover my whole slip. It wasn't missing much until Mike would have reached his goal. Just when he tried my slip, the door was thrown open again. Ellis and two men stormed the room. One pulled Mike off me by the shoulders while the other held his hands. Nonetheless, Mike had had the chance to hurt one of them on the arm. In the chaos, Ellis stormed to my side immediately and threw a blanket over me. She herself stood in front of me waving the blanket, so that I had no   (156) chance to see what was going on. It was sheer chaos. The two men manhandled Mike out the door and pulled him down the stairs. Outside, a loud discussion arose, which included the word "police" a few times and was accompanied by the hotel owner complaining about his guests. I was still shaking all over and now sobbing in Ellis's arms until I was completely worn out. Curled up, I lay on the bed, still wrapped in the blanket, when someone knocked very gently on the door. Ellis covered me with the blanket and secretly snuck to the door. She whispered behind her hand. Who with, I could not see, and neither did I recognise the voice. After a few seconds, she came back.

"Who was that?" I asked softly.

"Oh, I thought you were asleep. That! That was just David. He wanted to know how you were and tell you that that pig Mike is on a plane. There are huge charges waiting for him in Germany. If you bear witness. You... You will bear witness, won't you?" she asked. I only nodded in silence.

"Get some more rest," Ellis said. I sighed.

"Oh Ellis, all I want to do is shower and then I could use a glass of whiskey." My friend grinned at me and excitedly clapped her hands. (157)

"Yes, let's do that. The day after tomorrow is our last day anyway, but if you want, we can leave tomorrow already," she immediately allowed. But I shook my head.

"No, we don't have to," I said and could not help but shiver at the thought. She looked at me and just nodded. She knew that now I especially didn't want to go home. Sure, to be at home was different from a holiday, but the thought that I might meet Mike again made me shake for a moment. How would I treat him when I met him? What would he do? Surely he would have a thousand promises at the ready to apologise and tell me how sorry he was, but I did not want to see him again.

Chapter Eleven

I quickly grabbed a few things and went to have a long shower. Even though he hadn't raped me, I still felt dirty and ashamed. It was incomprehensible to me how Mike could to something like this and how far he had been willing to go. Between water and shower head, my tears flowed once again, but this time, they were tears of relief. Ten minutes later, I was done and freshened up. I put on new clothes and would have loved to throw the old ones away. For now, I just buried them at the bottom of my bag.

Freshly showered and dressed, I already felt better. Ellis wanted to take me downstairs to the in-house pub, but I did not want to go in there. It was all embarrassing enough. When we walked downstairs, I prayed that we wouldn't run into anyone. Sadly, the guy from the reception crossed our path. To my surprise, he looked at me and asked me how I was. I just nodded and said that all was okay and apologised for all the inconvenience. But the man waved me off and smiled.

"All will be fine. Believe me. I understand. Don't miss out on the good air and take a deep breath. All else will be fine eventually. Forget the guy, he's not worth it," he winked (159) at me and buried his nose in his computer again. Ellis linked arms with me and we marched out the door.

The weather was on our side. The sun shone through the clouds. It wasn't cold, but a gentle breeze was blowing. The air did me good. The salty sea air went deep into my lungs and I breathed again. Ellis also sucked in the air, but she lit a cigarette and shrugged guiltily.

"Stupid addiction," she laughed. I leaned against the door, remembering something.

"Say, who was there apart from David, by the way? I mean the person who pulled Mike away. And anyway, where were you all night?" Although I had a good idea. Ellis's eyes already told me where she had been. Before my friend could answer, she took a deep drag of her cigarette and immediately choked.

"I… erm, you know… Well…" She didn't get any further when she heard her David.

"Hey baby, how's it going? Oh hey, you're already up and about. We were all real worried. Man, this place is more exciting than home," he grinned and gave Ellis an enthusiastic kiss. She squeaked a little and looked at me almost guiltily. I waved her off. (160)

"Hey, hey, hey, may I seduce the ladies to try a real, tasty Irish Mist?" he asked and beamed at us. I just nodded. I didn't care, as long as it was high proof and dulled my emotions a bit. We were just crossing the street to wander down the promenade and across the famous Half Penny Bridge, which would lead us directly to Temple Bar, today's pub destination. That was the idea.

As we were just crossing the street, a few people came in the other direction. Suddenly, I felt a hand grab me. I got so frightened that I screamed, but somehow, the touch also felt familiar. Before I knew what was happening, I was looking into Kyran's eyes. Had he been crying or was it just the wind, I thought. His eyes were reddened. I looked over at Ellis and she immediately gave me a thumbs up and called out, "We'll see you at Temple Bar," and just like that, she floated away. On the one hand, I was glad to see him, but on the other hand I was a little dispirited and didn't know what I was supposed to say to him. Apparently, he felt the same way. Nonetheless, he grabbed my hand and pulled me with him to a bench. There, we looked straight at the water, which was softly sloshing back and forth. Food smells reached my nose, mingling with the smell of the salt. Kyran seemed to be fighting for his composure. He was sitting bent over and running his   (161) hands through his hair. Again and again. He sighed, struggling for words.

"I was such an idiot," he began and tore at his hair again. What else was I supposed to say to that. I had so many questions, but I was paralysed. I also didn't want to look at him. I was too ashamed. Has he heard anything of what happened with Mike, I wondered and stole a glance at him. It panged in my chest. And yet I couldn't let him go. Right when I wanted to address him to ask what was going on, my gaze fell on his arm. His jeans shirt had a small slit, which was drenched in blood. I felt hot and cold at the same time. Could it be? I looked at him and struggled for words. Then I grabbed the arm.

"Where did you get this?" I asked straight out. But I already knew the answer.

"How... I mean, why were you there?" I asked. Kyran tried to look at me, then it burst out of him.

"Oh Elara, I was such an idiot," he began. Yeah, we've done that already, I thought. "This is all my fault. The day you were going to leave, Dyllon filled me up, saying things like come on, bro, one more won't kill you. So I thought. Until I woke up the next morning with a hellish hangover. Either way,   (162)

I wanted to go straight to you at the airport, but it was too late. Then Dyllon started with these rumours. You were only here for fun, you met other people. The same evening, he surfed the web and said he found something I would find interesting. So he presented your husband Mike. With the status: Married and happy." Kyran was standing now and gesturing nervously.

"But the thing with Mike is…" I tried to interrupt, but Kyran didn't hear me.

"Don't you understand? I was so… oh, so hurt. Dyllon showed me the picture of you both arm in arm at the beach, and you looked so happy. Don't you get it, I really believed you were. Either way, Dyllon dragged me from appointment to appointment and left me no time. Photoshoots, advertisements, performances without a break. And for what?" He shrugged and looked at the water, then kicked a stone that was lying by the railing, which sank amidst gentle waves. I got up now and stood next to him. When he continued speaking, he didn't look at me. "When you were gone, not a second passed without me thinking of you. But the pictures haunted me and did not let me rest. I believed all the lies, and as time passed, I came to terms with them. Until the day you appeared at the pub." He looked so fragile that I felt like I needed to be near him. I wanted to touch his arm,   (163) touch him, but I was too afraid. So I left it alone and looked at him instead.

"That's why you blew me off. Why on earth didn't you say anything about this at the pub?" I barked at him. Now Kyran looked at me as well. His eyes looked so vulnerable, and it touched my very soul.

"Well, it's because after Dyllon saw you, he handed me his phone and your husband Mike answered. Goodness, he praised you and your relationship with him so highly and also that you were about to repeat your marriage vows. What was I supposed to believe?" Well, that seemed just like Mike, but to think Dyllon of all people would be capable of something like this was unexpected. Of course he had been mean and malicious towards me, but I had believed it to be out of fear for his career. A short silence fell, and when Kyran continued speaking I flinched involuntarily.

"Well, that evening I tried to forget you again. But even my sister and the alcohol didn't help much. Only after you were gone I finally understood that I had lost you. Or so I thought. I could have slapped myself." He squirmed and grieved a little. Nonetheless, he was now looking right at me. I could have melted, but when I thought back to him blowing me off (164) in that pub and finding consolation in the arms of another, I looked forlornly to the side.

"Oh, that's why you needed the distraction. I mean, I can relate. If someone told me that you... I mean, that there is someone else. Which there is. But what am I saying. As long as you are happy." Did I really mean that? Internally, it tore me apart, and on the outside, my voice was cracking a bit. Kyran on the other hand stared at me as if I had grown a second head.

"Happy? What are you talking about? I am trying to explain to you how much of an idiot I've been, and you say that I am happy." Kyran looked completely lost and to be honest, so was I. I twisted my fingers nervously. Had I said something wrong?

"I... What am I talking about? Well, even though it's none of my business anymore, I mean your girlfriend at the pub. The pretty brunette who kissed you. I mean... even if I don't trust Dyllon, but he also said that it was your..." I didn't get further. Kyran was laughing now and leaning over the railing, then he turned around again and looked at me. He gently took hold of my shoulder and his eyes shone. I didn't know whether it was with happiness or confusion or despair. Somehow,   (165)

I felt caught out. "What? What's there to laugh about?" I asked, bewildered and a little angry.

"You!" he laughed and looked at me softly. "You, Elara. Until today, I never knew you were jealous." Now I was really getting angry. Was this the revenge for Mike? Even though I still didn't have the full story. Especially how he ended up saving me from Mike. I wanted to turn away and pout a little, but Kyran kept looking at me.

"Yeah, just keep laughing at me," I said. But Kyran took my head in his hands and kissed me. I wanted to fend him off, but I didn't understand what was going on here.

"But... I... What?" I asked breathlessly. His grey-blue eyes bored into mine.

"Elara, Elara. That person in the pub was my sister. I know that to you it probably looked suspicious, but believe me, we just have a very close relationship. And we hadn't seen each other in a while. That's why we hugged and kissed. And concerning Dyllon, I believe he saw another chance to get one over on us. Which seems to have worked. Oh, Elara." He hugged me close and I had to put my thoughts in order. His sister? This had to be a joke. Kyran seemed to sense my insecurity and raised his hand. (166)

"Wait! I'll show you," he mumbled and fished his phone out of his pocket, then he swiped a few pages and opened his gallery.

"It's a little older, but this is at my mum's birthday. There, you see? Next to me is my sister, and look at the cake. It says: From your children Kyran and Michelle. Oh, come on, Elara, she really is my sister. What else am I supposed to do? Wait, I know. I'll call her," he said jauntily and started tapping around on his phone. Oh no, no, that was too embarrassing after all. I took his hand away.

"Alright, okay, I believe you," I tried to smile. Kyran looked at me.

"God, I missed you so much," he whispered very softly and kissed me again. Time stood still for me in the here and now. Was this how real happiness felt, but how should it go on? After a few seconds, we separated, or at least our lips, but Kyran was still holding me close. We stood here at the Liffey in the gentle sunshine, amidst the people hurrying past us. A babble of voices surrounded us. Cars drove down the street and a police car made its rounds. That caused me to continue my line of thought.

(167)

"How did you know I was in trouble at the hotel?" I asked him. He looked at me and nodded.

"Oh, right. Goodness, I didn't even get to that yet. So, that evening with my sister." He wagged his finger and smiled until I gently jabbed him in the ribs. "Alright, alright. So, that evening I tried to forget you once again, of course Dyllon helped me to the best of his ability and paid for with one whiskey after the other. After your appearance and disappearance, your friend Ellis came over to me. She was trying to tell me something, but my brain wasn't working right, so Sean, your Ellis, and some David grabbed me and forced several cups of coffee down my throat at a corner stall. Then they kept me going until the wee hours. Chased me up and down O'Connell Street until I was somewhat sober again. The rest of the night, we were stuck on Ha'penny Bridge and Sean told me everything about this Mike and Dyllon. I immediately took him to task and told him what I thought of him. Well, we shall see what I end up doing about him. After all, he isn't a bad guy and has loyally stood by me for years. Why he did what he did I don't know, but the last word hasn't been spoken in this matter. So now it was early morning and Ellis asked me to please try to talk to you. You would surely be at the hotel. So we went and well, you know the rest. Your friend really has a big mouth," he laughed and I laughed too. I was   (168) so glad about all that had happened, but I also had to realize with some horror that I would be back on a plane again two days from now and fly home. Kyran saw my face. "What are you thinking about?" he asked immediately and I just shrugged.

"I just don't know what I am supposed to do now. I mean, is everything really said between us now, and how shall we go on? You know I have to go home in two days," I said dejectedly. The young man immediately embraced me tightly, as if he never wanted to let me go again. We stood ten more minutes tightly intertwined, then he grabbed my hand.

"Whatever, let's get something to eat first. Then we'll see. I don't want to think about two days from now." Somewhat sad, but still determined, he took my hand and I just nodded. But internally, I was already thinking ahead and thought with pain of the coming goodbye. It was merely late morning and the sun was giving its all. Suddenly, Kyran got more hectic and grinned at me. "Wait here!" he commanded with a smile, kissed me, and disappeared around the corner of a side street for a moment. I had thankfully found a bench and sat down for the time being. I watched the goings-on on the street and found that they didn't affect me at all. In the past, I had always been the type to sit down feeling awkward, because I   (169) always believed that people were watching and laughing about me. But this time, I did the watching, with the difference that I wasn't laughing about people. I was thinking about life and goings-ons here in Dublin and in Ireland in general. It really was as people said. Whoever lives in Ireland or meets someone Irish learns to know and love the mentality and humour. Everyone was easy-going and really friendly. Not like in some other cities, arrogant and conceited and worried only about themselves. Pleased, I smiled to myself and was completely relaxed. The gentle breeze caressed my face. I closed my eyes and allowed the sunbeams to warm my face. No idea how much time had passed when a shadow appeared before me.

"Are you going to share those dreams with me?" asked Kyran and looked at me dreamily. I laughed. He held out his hand and motioned for me to accompany him. In his other hand, he held a bag that was rattling a little. We sauntered to his car and got in. A few streets down, we left Dublin. He took the road to Howth. We stopped at the harbour. When we got out, a stormy breeze met me which took my breath away at first. I turned to the side and it got better. Kyran took the lead along the harbour to a path that obviously led into the wilderness. We had to go up a long path, along which we met several people, but they were carrying backpacks and wore   (170) hiking boots. Which was definitely more comfortable. Not that I minded, but I wasn't prepared for longer walks like this. We kept going higher. I looked up and thought I could not go on much longer, and I was about to tell Kyran when we finally stopped at a cliff. The wind was blowing stronger now, but it freed all my thoughts. Up here, we had an amazing view over the ocean. On our right, I saw a white lighthouse and the waves crashing against the small boulders so hard that they foamed. On our left was the long, stretched-out bay poking out of the harbour. A few boats were anchored at sea, and a few people were running around on the beach. Kyran unfolded a blanket and made two glasses appear, along with a bottle of whiskey, two lots of pasties, and strawberries. He must have quickly grabbed all these in a supermarket in Dublin. We sat down and enjoyed the taste of the whiskey. Kyran looked at me and smiled.

"What?" I asked and laughed as well. He came over to me and sat down behind me so I could cuddle against him.

"Doesn't this seem familiar to you?" he asked me and quickly kissed my neck. A shiver ran through me. I closed my eyes for a moment.

"Oh, yes, I remember. I think we were sitting here last time."

He turned me around so that I was sitting on his lap. "This is where I kissed you for the first time," he whispered, and then his lips were on mine. I hadn't realised how much I had missed it. Almost forgotten were Mike and also Ellis and David and the whole holiday. Held in a tight embrace, we sat here on the blanket and let the day pass by. It wasn't until the late afternoon that the weather got worse. Dark clouds appeared and at the firmament I could hear faraway thunder. Kyran glanced up.

"I think we should probably get going, it is going to get really unpleasant here really soon," he said and pointed at the horizon. I nodded, even though it was a pity. Today and here I had felt exceedingly good after what had happened with Mike. With Kyran's help, I reluctantly got up. He pulled me up by my arms and I let myself fall into his. I didn't want to let him go, but the thunder was coming closer. Even before we had collected the remnants of our picnic, a cloudburst came down. As quickly as we could, we ran back to the car and got in, already soaking wet. Kyran ran a hand through his wet hair ,and I involuntarily thought back to the moment when we were in his house. Kyran laughed and shook himself like a dog afterwards. I also had to laugh now, until he suddenly slapped a hand to his forehead.

(172)

"Oh, I'm an idiot," he called out and looked at me guiltily.

"What? What happened?" I asked immediately. Had I done something wrong again? But Kyran made puppy eyes at me.

"Oh, I am so sorry, but in this weather and especially with the thunder Jimmy always goes wild." Well, I could understand that. I just nodded.

"If you want, I'll bring you back to your hotel while I look after him and then come pick you up again." I had no idea what he meant by that or what I was supposed to think. Did it look like he wanted to get rid of me? Somewhat irritated, I turned away and played awkwardly with my hair.

"Okay, if you think so," I just said stubbornly. But Kyran was already looking at me.

"You... you are mad," he asserted and looked at me again right away, all while putting an arm around me and looking at me with a smile. "Oh... Oh no, I... Oh goodness gracious, I didn't mean to offend you. It's just that... I thought you might not want to come over to my place because... you know, Mike." He was completely flustered now.

"No. No, I really don't mind. Did you think Mike had brought me to my knees with that?" I asked him, but Kyran didn't know how to respond.

"Well, I thought. Oh, I don't know either what I thought," he tried to defend himself, but I just hugged him quickly and gave him a kiss.

"Come on, don't let poor Jimmy suffer any longer. We can put him in the car and then you can bring me to the hotel. I…" My voice broke and I had to swallow. Kyran looked at me questioningly.

"What?" he asked immediately. But I shook my head. "Elara, please, what is it?" he needled me and looked at me pleadingly.

"I have to start packing my bags," I said sadly. Kyran looked at me, shocked and hurt at the same time. He had forgotten about it as well. We were silent for a while, until a flash of lightning lit up the sea and the following thunder split the heavens.

"Let's go!" I said to him and Kyran nodded, relieved. He quickly started the engine and we went back to Dublin. Since his house was closer than the hotel we went there.   (174)

My clothes were wet, but it was nothing that couldn't be dried off with a towel. And anyway, what did it matter if I possibly had to dress in one of his shirts, after all, he knew me well enough without clothing.

When we reached the house, we already heard a whining and yowling from inside. Jimmy was wildly scratching at the door. I did feel sorry for him. Kyran also tried to hurry and quickly got out.

"Wait, I'll help you," I said and also got out. Kyran just nodded. When we reached the front door, he stopped for a moment.

"We have to hurry. As soon as I open the door, he will try to get away. And believe me, he'll be ruthless. If I don't manage to grab him right away, he'll be running back and forth through the city, maybe even onto the street. So if you really want to help me, then please try to grab his collar, but don't let him bite you." He winked at me. I nodded and gently jabbed him. I had to admit the small fear that Jimmy could snap in a panic. Kyran carefully unlocked the door and stayed in a slightly bent position.

"Hey, Jimmy, my boy, it's me," he called through the door. Whining and yowling was the reply. I could already see the poor dog zip past me. Then I remembered (175) something. I quickly dashed back to the car and grabbed a piece of pastry. Maybe hunger would win out, I thought and pressed it into Kyran's hand. He looked at me, clearly confused.

"No thanks, I am not hungry right now," he said dryly and I had to laugh.

"Not for you. For Jimmy, as a distraction."

Now he got it. "Oh, yes, sure. Great idea," he just said and gave me a quick kiss before he opened the door wider. He quickly held the meaty dough out in front of him. I felt like I was in a scene on feeding crocodiles, and Kyran was the keeper. Hey, just a moment, what did that make me? As a second watchman, erm, watchwoman I walked after him. As soon as the door was open, Jimmy jumped towards us. At the last moment, Kyran managed to grab his collar, and I quickly closed the door. As I did, I squatted down and looked deep into Jimmy's eyes. Why I did that I couldn't say myself. I think I had seen it on TV before, basically like some kind of dog whisperer. Either way, I tried it. I looked at him and whispered to him.

"Sshhh, my boy, all is good. All is fine. Calm down, nothing will happen to you, calm down." And again and again, "calm, boy". I noticed that he really was getting calmer, until   (176) his nose slowly touched my arm and he rested his head lightly in the crook of my elbow. He was panting and shaking a little. Kyran stood there with his mouth open.

"How?" he asked, but I just shrugged.

"When I was a kid, I used to have a dog, but that was a long time ago."

Kyran nodded, quickly walked into the kitchen and rummaged in a drawer, then he got Jimmy's bowl and filled it with fresh food as well as a substance. I looked at him imploringly.

"The vet gave me this. Tranq drops. He said it was for the best. But I couldn't foresee that the weather would turn so quickly," he explained and I laughed.

"We are in Ireland," I said dryly and Kyran grinned back. We both accompanied the poor dog to his bowl, which he at first eyed skeptically. Only when I put a piece on my hand he sniffed it and took a bite. I sat down next to the bowl and tapped it continuously. Reluctantly, he took another bite. Only when Kyran sat down next to us, Jimmy ate everything. We leaned against the wall.

"How long does it take for the drops to work?" I asked. (177)

"Oh, it can be different. Sometimes they work quickly, sometimes more slowly, but we'll find out soon. If you want, you can go and freshen up," he said and pointed at the bathroom. I just nodded.

"It's not really like it matters anymore now," I smiled and shook my hair a little, which was already beginning to dry. My clothes were still pretty damp, which was not exactly comfortable. So we spent the next minutes sitting on the cold hallway floor and slowly, something was happening to Jimmy. He no longer whined quite as loudly and crawled closer to me. I petted him and felt his breathing, which was slowing down. Another five minutes later I could finally get up, for which my bones thanked me. Jimmy had fallen asleep. Kyran also got up and walked over to the fireplace.

"I'm afraid if I don't light this now we'll be wet forever." It felt a bit absurd to turn on the fireplace in the middle of summer, but perhaps it wasn't such a bad idea. My body felt cold. Kyran put a few logs on the fireplace and in no time, a flame was flickering. He rubbed his hands together and was about to get a towel, but I held on to his arm. He turned to face me and I looked into his grey-green eyes, which transfixed me. I didn't know what it was, but something about him pulled me in. He put a hand to the back of my head and pulled me closer. (178)

Then he gently laid his lips on mine. I returned the kiss demandingly. We were both standing by the fireplace. Before I knew what I was doing, I pulled off my sweater. I pushed Kyran gently to the sofa, which he let himself fell onto. I sat on top of him and kissed him passionately while I got rid of my undershirt as well. He looked at me, a question in his eyes.

"Are you sure you want this?" he asked me hoarsely. I just nodded and unbuttoned his shirt. While doing so, I kept kissing his chest over and over. His breathing sped up. He now had his hands on my back and I got rid of all my upper layers. He also took off his shirt and undershirt. I got up for a moment to pull off my trousers while he took off his. I sat back on top of him and he moaned. His lips covered my upper body while I dug my hands into his hair. I swayed back and forth and heard his breathing quicken. He was writhing with me on the sofa until his hands held my back and he put me on my back. I nonchalantly put one leg on the backrest of the sofa and let the other dangle loosely, so that my legs were spread and he could lie between them. He kissed me passionately and we rocked in the act of love and passion.

Chapter Twelve

Tightly entwined, we stayed there until the late evening. The thunderstorm had slowly moved on and left behind a steady rain. My clothes were dry now, and even Jimmy was starting to stir. While I sat like that, I memorised Kyran's face. He was sleeping sweetly. To look at him sent a pang to my soul. To know that I had to leave tomorrow... How would things continue between us? Would they continue at all? A small tear escaped my eyes, and I was about to brush it away when I felt his hand on my cheek.

"What is it?" he asked softly and dozily. I shook my head and cuddled back up to his chest. His breath was calming to me and his scent made my thoughts run in circles. The farewell was looming so close and it frightened me. Of course I had a life in Germany, but the thought of Mike scared me. I would have to see him eventually. So caught up in my thoughts I didn't even hear the phone ring. Kyran heard it, but didn't answer it. After a while, the answerphone cut in. It was Dyllon.

"Jesus, Kyran. I am so sorry. I really didn't mean for this to happen. Come on, buddy, don't make me beg. We've always been such a good team. You surely don't want to throw (180) this all away. Hey, I mean, if she means that much to you, okay, but please let us talk. Why don't you come to the pub tonight. Just for one Guinness. Kyran? Damn..." Beep, he'd hung up. Kyran grinned a little and kissed the top of my head.

"He's always been a silly billy," he said and I looked up at him.

"But if you've been together this long, I mean you and your band. Maybe he really deserves a second chance. And also, once I leave again, it'll all be forgotten anyway and you don't need to worry anymore. Trust your heart and keep your musical family together. Talk to him," I said and almost didn't understand myself. What was I saying? If it was up to me, I would happily strangle the guy myself. Alright, on the other hand I could understand him, even if it was just the tiniest bit.

Kyran tried to prop himself up a little while looking at me and shook his head. Very quietly and with a choked-off voice, he whispered, "I don't want you to go. Stay with me!" He took my head in his hands, pulled me down to him and kissed me as if there was no tomorrow. His body was warm, not to say hot. I felt his erection, but he suddenly got to his feet and pulled me along by the hand.

"Come on!" he said and moved towards the bedroom. Once there, he gently laid me down amidst the silk pillows   (181) and lay down next to me. A small night light was glowing and giving off just enough light for me to see the silhouette of his face. But after a few minutes, I had gotten used to the light and saw him lie next to me. His eyes beamed at me, full of longing. I tried to meet his gaze, but I didn't manage it without losing some of my tears. He put his arms around me and pulled me close. We just lay there like that and listened to the rain drum on the roof, which was calming, as I found. I was about to say something when his finger touched my lips, insinuating that I should stay quiet. So I stayed silent. Instead, I took his hand and kissed his fingers, while he pulled me closer with his other hand. I could feel his passion and skillfully rolled on top of him.

While I sat on top of him cross-legged, he took hold of my head and kissed me passionately. His lips wandered down to my curves. I reared up a little and elicited a moan from him. Only slowly at first, I swayed back and forth, only to continue in the rhythm of passion until we reached the climax and exhaustedly fell into the pillows. Nonetheless, he kept hold of me the whole time. The evening had begun and it was only drizzling now, but the night was pitch black. The occasional headlights of passing cars threw odd reflections on the wall. We fell asleep peacefully and tightly entwined, and when I awoke, my watch showed two in the morning.   (182)

I stealthily slipped out of his grip and put on one of his shirts. Then I walked to the window, which went all the way to the ground, and carefully opened it. A gentle breeze wafted around me. The rain smelled so fresh and the cool air did me a world of good. From afar I could see a few lights from other houses, while outside the door, a few cars could be heard. A couple of young men walked the walk home from the pub, slightly intoxicated, and were talking loudly. But their voices faded the further they went. I sucked in the air and wrapped my arms around my body. I was feeling a bit chilly, but I didn't mind. Kyran's shirt smelled so much of him that I crossed my arms even more. I could hear soft grunting from the living room. Jimmy was snoring. When I thought about it, Mike had always had a full-throated snore, but here, all I could hear was Jimmy. A smile hushed across my face, only for my eyes to stare longingly into the distance. What had I expected, or was expecting now?

"Penny for your thoughts," Kyran whispered behind me and wrapped me up in a hug. He kissed my hair and wandered down my neck. I wanted to turn around, but Kyran held me tight. His hands went further and further down to my lust centre. There they halted for a moment before they kept working away. I cursed and moaned at the same time. He teased me mercilessly, so that I had to clasp my hands (183) to my mouth so I wouldn't scream out loud. Only then he turned me around and my body leaned against the window wall. He lifted me up and finished with his own needs his way. Dizzy with ecstasy, we fell into each other's arms. The air brought a little drizzle in to us and made our skin sparkle. I don't remember how we got back to bed, only that once there, we continued our game of love until the early hours of the morning.

The sun tickled my nose when I woke. I stretched and noticed that Kyran wasn't there. My clothes were still scattered in the living room, so I snuck down the hall on tiptoes. But why, I thought and had to giggle a little. Had I expected him to be here and make breakfast? Far from it, he wasn't there, even though the coffee machine was running. A pan was on the stove, but it wasn't on. Cheese and jam waited on the counter alone with two mugs, butter, and orange juice. Searching for him, I looked around. Kyran wasn't in the bathroom either, and outside? I peeked through the window and startled; a man stared at me, his face red. That was when the scales fell from my eyes. I was still naked and shamefully exposing my upper body to the postman. Embarrassing. I squeaked and disappeared behind the curtain. The man simply smiled and nodded at me approvingly, before leaving with a whistle. Apparently I had made his day a bit sweeter.   (184)

I quickly collected my clothes before I could end up with another surprise. In the bathroom I had a quick wash and made the bed, all the while grinning like a lovestruck teenager. From outside, I heard a dog bark and a key move in the lock. Kyran came in, wearing a tracksuit and carrying a paper bag of soda bread and scones.

"Hey, sweet one, I got breakfast." He gave me a kiss and put the things down. I looked at him happily until the phone rang again. Kyran didn't answer, instead waiting for the answerphone again.

"Hi Kyran, this is Sean. I, um, really just wanted to ask if you possibly know where Elara is. Her friend Ellis and David have already been looking for her. Their plane leaves soon, and they have to get out of the hotel. Oh, and I am supposed to ask you if and when you are going to sound recordings again? Erm, Dyllon wanted to know. Right, so, that's it. I… urgh, I hate these things. Doesn't anyone have a working mobile anymore. Oh damn, it's still recording." Bam, the phone fell silent. Oh God, I slapped a hand to my forehead.

"Oh dear, I completely forgot about Ellis. The poor woman is about to end up on the street with packed suitcases. I need to check out and I need to get to the airp--" I didn't go on. Kyran's face twisted into a heap of misery. For a few   (185) seconds, all that could be heard was silence. The only sound came from Jimmy's drooling as he greedily slobbered around in his bowl after his and Kyran's walk to the bakery. I awkwardly pulled at my scone. I had lost my appetite anyway, and evidently, Kyran felt the same.

"Then I'd better put on some clothes and drive you to the hotel," he muttered and disappeared in the bedroom. Moments later, he returned neatly dressed. He filled his dog's bowl one more time and grabbed the car keys. Just before he reached the door, he stopped again and lowered his head, then he turned around and took my head in his hands again. He looked at me with his grey-green eyes. They were shiny. Were they holding tears? He pressed his forehead against mine. "Please stay!" he begged. I felt dizzy. I was shaking a little, which was also noticeable in my voice.

"Oh, Kyran, what is it you want me to do? I mean, how is this supposed to work? How long should I stay? I mean, my holiday is over in three days," I whined. Oh please, Elara, do you really think he meant that, I scolded myself, and the little devil on my shoulder flipped me the bird while the little angel on my other looked at me with pity. Kyran looked straight at me. He kissed me briefly and said what I hadn't wanted to voice.

(186)

"Holiday? Elara, I want you to stay completely. Don't you understand? I want to see you every day, feel you every day. Argue with you, laugh and cry with you. Feel you. Oh Elara, stay with me forever. Please!" he sighed. And I had to swallow, feeling the first beginnings of goosebumps. I tried to hold back my tears, but they just flowed out of me. Why did it all have to be so complicated. But there was no helping it. Either way, I had to go to the hotel first. We let go of each other with difficulty and got in the car, and for the whole trip he held my hand whenever possible. When we got to the hotel, Ellis was already standing outside with David and was arguing with the hotel manager.

"Oh Goodness gracious, Elara, finally. Say, have you lost your mind? I am waiting here and have to argue with this… this… oh, nevermind. Either way you could have at least gotten in touch or answered your phone. What were you doing all this time, anyway?" Ellis vented. But when she saw Kyran, she looked back at me and saw how I sheepishly lowered my head. Ellis grinned widely and pinched David's side.

"Aah, so that's how the wind blows. Who would have thought." Kyran rubbed my back for a moment and took the hotel manager aside. He talked to him very quickly and nodded every now and again, then he handed him a business card and they shook hands. Shortly after, he came back over to us.

"It's all done. If you have anything still in the room you can go get it now," he said, but Ellis shook her head.

"Nah, I tossed everything that was still strewn around and belonged to us into the suitcase," she grouched and turned to David.

"Oh babe, I'm afraid this is farewell. Come here!" she demanded and jumped into his arms, all while kissing every part she could reach. The people around us were already watching in amusement. Kryan quickly took my hand and squeezed it. I felt so helpless. David on the other hand just grinned.

"Hey man, stay cool, I already thought of something. I mean, I'm still travelling and hey, what can I say, I could definitely imagine a trip to Germany."

Ellis stared at him. "You mean you… you would come with me?" David nodded and she threw her arms around him, screaming. The lump in my throat grew bigger again, so I avoided looking at Kyran, but he took my hand again and held it so tightly that it was almost painful. (188)

"So what are we waiting for? The plane is on time," Ellis cheered and grabbed her suitcase. She was already moving towards O'Connell Street to wait for the bus.

"Hey, leave it, I'll take you. Jump in!" Kyran said and opened his boot. Ellis grinned and David gave a thumbs-up.

"Hey, super cool, dude," and he got in the back with Ellis. I helped with the suitcases. He was just lifting my case and hesitated for a moment. He looked at me with a plea in his eyes.

"Please, Elara, stay! At least think about it," he said and his face looked so pained. I gently squeezed his hand and also got in the car. Throughout the car ride, Ellis and David kept whispering, snogging, and kissing in the back seat, while icy silence dominated the front. Time and again, Kyran took my hand when the opportunity presented itself and stroked it gently. Even though I welcomed this with a tingle, I felt absolutely lousy. After about ten miles the sign for the airport appeared. Now Kyran looked for a parking space and then we could go in. People were milling about like in an anthill. Everyone was running in every direction. Managers to suits, commuter to tourist. We had to do our check-in and then had two more hours until our flight departed. David had   (189) gotten his hands on a boarding pass at the last minute, because someone had unexpectedly cancelled. He and Ellis kept incessantly whispering sweet nothings to each other as we waited. Me and Kyran took a short wander through the terminal, past the Guinness store and the candy shop. The weather was now somewhat sunny to cloudy, but unlike last night it was dry. Last night, I remembered and a shiver ran down my body. In a quieter terminal we sat down on a bench. We were silently regarding one another. His forehead touched mine and his arms were wrapped around my back. I hardly dared to breathe. When he kissed me, the world around us disappeared. Only reluctantly we separated, but there was still that nagging uncertainty. How would this go on?

"I'll call you every day. And if you want, we can skype every day," he whispered and tried to smile. I felt queasy. I didn't want to leave him, but there was no other way. What about my work, about Ellis. What would happen between them? And most importantly, I essentially didn't really know Kyran. Could there be such a thing as love at first sight? I was usually a great doubter when it came to things like that, but this proved to be the exception. I could only sob and my tears were flowing with the pain of farewell. Our flight was called. I separated myself from him with great reluctance. He hugged me one more time and I kissed him passionately.   (190)

I could already hear Ellis's voice calling for me. It was high time. I asked him not to come all the way to the gate and Kyran simply nodded. So there I was with my little suitcase, waiting for my departure.

Chapter Thirteen

On the plane, I thought everything over once again and it felt so surreal. Nonetheless, I could still feel his body on mine. His kiss, his lips, and his scent. The flight passed quickly and welcomed me back to reality. So now I was home again. Ellis immediately went for her flat with David and I greeted my empty flat. A heap of mail had accumulated, but I ignored it for now. I put my suitcase in a corner and curled up on the sofa. I merely kept tight hold of my phone, hoping that Kyran would call or text. My senses had not betrayed me. At just that moment, Kyran wrote:

"Hey, my sweet one. I miss you already. Every moment, every second. Hope you got home safe. Love you." He had added numerous kiss emojis. I pressed the phone to my chest and cried silently for a while.

The ringing of the doorbell tore me out of my sleep. I had fallen asleep on the sofa and was still wearing my travel clothes. Sleepy and groggy I answered the door.

"Goodness gracious, look at you! Haven't you slept yet? What's wrong?" Ellis stormed past me. Of course she had David in her wake. He immediately started snooping around the flat.

"Oh wow, bad karma in here," he said and immediately threw open the windows, then he turned and pushed a few pieces of furniture. Ellis grinned, lovestruck.

"Isn't he unique?" she sighed and stared at her eco-fanatic David, full of love. Then she turned back to me. "Goodness gracious, Elara, what's up with you? Kyran?" she asked immediately and I burst into tears. Ellis looked slightly shocked, then she looked to David. He was still busy moving the furniture.

"Sweetheart, would you mind if us ladies went to the bathroom for a moment? You can run riot in here if you like. Kisses," she purred and blew him a kiss. He smiled and clicked his fingers.

"Yeah, that's real cool, babe," he said and attacked my CD shelf. Ellis pushed me to the bathroom and brought a bottle of whiskey from the living room cabinet along. In the bathroom, she sat me on the rim of the tub and poured me a large whiskey in a toothbrush cup.

"Alright, what's going on?" Ellis asked immediately and took a long swig from the bottle. I was still crying and, (193) accompanied by sobs and stutters, I told her of Kyran and his plan, or rather what he intended to do. After the stuttering there was silence, and Ellis's mouth was hanging open. She took another swig and grinned at me.

"Goodness gracious, don't you know how lucky you are? Man, you don't get men like that everywhere. He really loves you," she gushed, but I could not share in her enthusiasm.

"Oh, come on, Ellis, what am I supposed to do? Where should I work, and who even says that it will work out with him? No, that's all just fiction. A love that is no more. So forget it!" I said, but I had misjudged Ellis. Now she turned it up to eleven.

"Dear God, Elara, here you are meeting the love of your life and you doubt it? Goodness," she complained. But it was no use. It was too late. I cried without restraint.

I didn't come to until the next morning and realised that I was in bed. Ellis, or maybe even eco-freak David, had brought me there. I really hoped that it had just been Ellis who had undressed me. Either way I woke up with a headache once again. I experienced my life to be exactly the same as when I thought he had just used me. There was this emptiness again, and yet a feeling that was spreading in my chest.

I quickly showered and got dressed. In the kitchen, I found a note from Ellis.

"Have a nice day. And cheer up. We are coming over tonight to celebrate. Gotta tell you something. Kisses, E."

Well, at least Ellis had found her happiness. I was genuinely happy for her. Even if I thought eco-freak David was a bit odd.

Ellis wanted to go to the pub in the evening. Oh dear, was I even up for that? Who knew what she was planning this time. Potentially hook me up with someone so I would forget Kyran? But I didn't want to forget him, rather I wanted to know what my future with him would bring. Which brought me straight to my phone. My fingers flew over the keys to check my messages. My heart was racing. Another message from Kyran.

"My sweet El, I miss you. Love you, miss you."

My heart swelled and I quickly texted him back. This time I could approach the day with a small smile.

I got a lot of things done, such as grocery shopping, cleaning, and eating. In the evening I could already hear Ellis's laughter when she drove up to the house with David.

(195)

As soon as she was in the hallway, I unlocked the door and Ellis hugged me exuberantly.

"Hey, you look much better already," she told me and pressed a bottle of sparkling wine in my hand. David immediately slouched on the sofa and opened a can of beer. Ellis perched on the armrest and wrapped her arms around him. "So, shall we go?" she said right away. I really didn't feel like it, but I knew that she wouldn't let it go until I agreed. So I shrugged and grabbed my jacket. Ellis clapped excitedly. Since they both had already had a drink and Ellis pointed out that I would drink something as well, we took the last bus into town. We approached the small bistro which had Guinness on the tap. The outside tables were decorated with tealights and small vases with roses again. Everyone ordered a large pint of Guinness and we clinked glasses.

"To Ireland," Ellis said and we clinked again. My thoughts went to Kyran for a moment, and I raised a mental toast to him. David was fidgeting like a young puppy. He kept nudging Ellis, who hissed defensively.

"Alright, what's going on?" I asked my friend, and she knew that this time I wouldn't stop until I got it out of her. She hemmed and hawed, but then she started beaming and came out with it.   (196)

"Fine, fine. I'll be quick. David and I have decided to keep travelling the globe. We will pick places and work here and there, and who knows, maybe we will end up in Dublin again one day. David found a small hostel there, which is looking for a leaseholder for next year. Well, what can I say, David is already on the list."

That made an impact. I was shocked, but happy at the same time. Ellis had always been a bird of paradise. Nowhere could hold her for long, at least when it came to work. She was everywhere and nowhere, but always managed to pay her rent and live the good life. My friend looked at me.

"Oh, sweetie, I am sorry. I didn't mean to snub you. Hey, how about you just come along? Fine, you'd have to wait a year, but then... hey, then you can see Kyran," she beamed. Even though the offer sounded amazing, I thought to myself that Ellis must have lost it. That was probably David's influence. Of course the thought was there, but the execution seemed to be the problem to me. Either way, after that revelation nothing kept Ellis and David in town much longer. Only one week later they broke off their tents and went off to new shores. Their first destination was Denmark. David said that he really wanted to see the long sandy beaches and feel freedom under his feet. My mood was low. I had known my friend (197) since eighth grade. She had always been this erratic. Still, it was not easy for me to say goodbye. At the train station, we separated in tears.

"Oh Elara, I will send you a picture from each place we visit. Don't hang your head, we'll see each other again in one year max. Come here and let me hug you again," said, done.

David also came over to me, mimed a quick hug, and clicked his fingers at me. "Hey, you're also really rad for a girl," he grinned and they both boarded the train. So here I stood and watched my friend make her way in the world. I on the other hand was trying to fight my way back into my own life.

Chapter Fourteen

The days dragged on and I was busy with work. Kyran and I kept writing every day. But one day, my screen stayed empty. At first I didn't think much of it, after all he may just be busy, but three days later I still had no messages. During the weekend, I couldn't stand it anymore. I started texting him and tried to call. Nothing! He didn't answer his phone and my messages didn't get through. Was his phone broken? That had to be it, I thought. Nonetheless, I went to work feeling uneasy. I monotonously put off my work all day. Customers with questions only got short, clipped responses, much to the chagrin of my boss. Somehow, I managed to get the day over with. Just before closing, I was just getting rid of a few boxes when a colleague called for me over the speakers. I actually didn't feel at all like customers or price questions, much less overtime, but I put up a brave front, or so I thought. As soon as I was at the register, my colleague gave me a wide grin.

"There's a customer who wants to have an Irish whiskey. It's still in the back. Would you be a dear?" she purred and looked at me all dreamily. What was up with her? Just so that I could finally call it a day, I quickly ran back to our storage. I looked around. What was the customer thinking.   (199)

Then I reflected.

We didn't sell any Irish whiskey. My brow wrinkled and I tried to find this customer. That was easy. Nobody was around. Typical, it wasn't the first time that a customer asked for something and then thought better of it at the last second. I pulled the large rolling gate closed and wanted to go back to my colleague. Suddenly, a customer addressed me. He was half hidden behind a milk shelf and I could only hear a voice.

"Entschuldigen Sie, aber mein Whisky," he said in very broken German. Goosebumps went down my arms. It couldn't be. I had to see this guy. When I turned around, I looked straight into two grey-green eyes beaming back at me. My heart nearly stopped. In front of me really was Kyran. I held a hand to my mouth so I wouldn't scream, but it didn't help. Screaming, I threw my arms around his neck, until I realised that everyone was staring at me. Only my colleague was laughing cheekily. She had known about him. He had quickly let her in on his plan and was now standing in front of me.

"What... what are you doing here? I tried to reach you. How...?" I asked agitatedly, but Kyran took me back in his arms and pressed a passionate kiss to my lips. I was completely out of breath and really stumped.

"Surprise!" he just said and happily lifted me in his arms.(200)

"I just couldn't stand it without you anymore," he said and didn't want to let go of me again. I quickly clocked out and made my way out of that shop before anyone could comment. Outside, we regarded each other and I still couldn't quite believe it.

"Come," I just said and pulled him along. I grabbed my bike and pushed it to my flat. Thankfully it wasn't too far. On the way, I told him all about Ellis and David and their plans.

"Wow, that sounds great, but one year. Elara, as you can see I can hardly make it for a couple of months without you," he said and looked at me. I stopped for a moment.

"Let's go to my place first. I have to get changed and freshen up a bit, then we can go out for dinner and talk," I said and pressed a kiss to his cheek. Once at my flat, I locked my bike and we went in. He looked around.

"Nice place you got," he grinned and looked at me challengingly.

"What?" I asked immediately, and he walked over to me and grinned again. He took me in his arms and kissed me passionately. I didn't feel too good about it, since I was still wearing my work clothes. But that didn't matter to him. (201)

He kept kissing me and his hands went under my sweater. When he whispered to me, his voice was hoarse.

"Where is your bedroom?" He grinned. I just indicated with my head where to go, but we didn't make it there. My work clothes flew straight across the living room. And Kyran's clothes were scattered similarly across the whole room. Between bedroom and living room, we lay on the carpet and consummated our passion. Tightly curled around each other, we lay naked between the doors. I had to laugh and was so glad to have him with me. Half an hour later I got up from the uncomfortable position.

"I think I'll have a quick shower now. Get comfortable, it won't take long." I bent down one more time and kissed him. Kyran grinned and slapped my bum. Then I disappeared in the bathroom. When I came back, Kyran was laying in my bed and slumbering peacefully. He was stretched out and naked on top of the covers.

I looked at him in silence. His outlines, his muscles, and even the fine hairs on his body. His dark locks stuck up wildly and he was breathing evenly. I was breathing in his scent when I caught myself leaning against the doorframe, dreamily closing my eyes and smiling. After all, I was thinking back to when we met and to our first night. A shiver ran through me and   (202)

I felt his hands on my body, until I realised that they really were his. Kyran had gotten up and was standing in front of me. Now he was stroking my form and kissed it, then he wrapped his arms around my hips and ripped down my towel, in which I had still been wrapped, and directed me to the bed. He gently put me down on the sheets and looked at me. His hands ran through my hair and he whispered to me.

"Elara. Come with me and stay with me. I love you," then he kissed me again and our bodies merged like never before. A wave of passion swept through us and made us melt into one. Tightly entangled, we lay on the bed, and neither of us dared to say a word. Only our breathing was audible. After several minutes of silence, I put my chin on his chest so that my face was tilted a bit towards him. My fingers were playing with his short chest hair while he stroked my back.

"How did you even get the idea to come here without saying a word?" I asked him. He glanced at me.

"I already told you. I couldn't stand another minute without you." Then he sat up a little and took me in his arms, all while looking deep into my eyes. "I want you to come with me to my place and stay with me, don't you understand? I know we haven't known each other for long, but I feel like we have known each other forever. All I know is that I don't want (203) to live a single day without you." He kissed me again and I was genuinely touched. Nonetheless, doubts arose.

"I… I do understand what you mean. I feel the same, but what do you mean, I should come with you? To Ireland?" I asked and looked at him.

Kyran nodded excitedly. "Yes, sweet love, of course to Ireland," he smiled.

"Kyran, how do you think that will work? I mean, where should I live and work, and what if we do fight after all or even break up, what then?" My head was spinning and my thoughts were racing through a life in Ireland and with him. Kyran grinned.

"Of course you'll live with me and Jimmy, and when it comes to work I am sure you'll find something. Oh Elara, please think about it. Please, come with me!" he begged again. I was a bit overwhelmed. The temptation was huge.

"Don't be mad, but… I think I need some time to think about this," I told him and he understood. We spent the rest of the day in bed. Around evening time, hunger finally forced us out. We went and had a good time in a restaurant. Kyran ordered a large stake with potato wedges and a salad, while I went for a schnitzel with mushroom sauce and chips. Afterwards, (204) we spent a few hours in the small bistro with the Guinness from the tap. Kyran was very taken by the small bistro and he felt very much at home. That evening we drank a lot, laughed and talked. The hours spun on and I only remembered late and with sudden fear that I had work in the morning. Ellis would now tell me to call in sick, but I wasn't the type to do that. So I gritted my teeth and motioned for Kyran to make our way home. He also looked visibly tired and agreed. In my flat we took off our clothes and lay down next to each other just like that until we were both asleep. In this context I have to say that I wasn't usually the type to like having a man next to me. Back when, Mike used to snore so loud that I spent many a night on the sofa. But here I had to say that was not an issue. Even when I met Kyran and spent the night there, this hadn't been the case. Rather the opposite, it was even calming to lay there with him like that.

The morning of course was all the worse for it. I had barely closed my eyes when the alarm went off. But there was no helping it. I had to get up. Work called unavoidably. I quickly put on a pot of coffee and set the table for Kyran, then I jetted to work. Even if customers were at their most annoying, today I found a smile and an open ear for each and every one of them. During my break, I chatted to my colleague who had been there when Kyran got to her register.   (205)

She started to gush about how lucky I was. But I felt introspective and told her about the plans and my doubts. Usually, this wasn't very me, since it was Ellis's job to listen to me, but sadly she wasn't here and I hadn't heard anything from her either. My colleague listened patiently. Then she grabbed a coffee and ate a cookie with it. She permanently dunked it into her cup. While I was studying my shift plan, Marianne, my colleague, began talking about another colleague. I knew it was impolite, but I was only half listening. When she told me that I should try it, since after all the colleague had been transferred right away, I finally started listening.

"Oh, I'm really sorry, but I was deep in thought. What do you mean, transferred?" I therefore asked again. Marianne grinned.

"Oh Elara, all I've heard so far about you and your Kyran sounds like a fairy tale. I am just saying, if you want, you can get transferred to Ireland. We have enough branches there, all you have to do is talk to the boss. Believe me, he's open for everything." She grinned and put her mug down and left, all while winking and giving me a thumbs-up. Why hadn't I thought of that. There had been several cases of colleagues transferring to another branch. Last I heard was a   (206) colleague who went to northern Germany, to the coast. But Ireland was a whole nother kettle of fish. Well, Marianne was right, I had to try. Luckily I knew that our boss would come in later that afternoon, so I decided to talk to him right away.

Work until then had never been as easy as that day. I was already counting the minutes until Mr Hendriks would come in. Thankfully, he was in a good mood as well. So I took the chance. I knocked and he immediately asked me in.

"Oh, hello, what can I do for you?" he asked immediately and I began to explain my situation and brought forward my request as well. His face was growing thoughtful now and I had bad forebodings.

"Well, that sounds really lovely for you, but I am afraid my reach does not extend all the way to Ireland. As much as I regret to say it." He looked at me apologetically and I just nodded. Either way, it had been worth a try. Despite the shame I grit my teeth and smiled.

"Oh, that's not a problem. It was just a silly thought. Thank you anyway." I nodded and went back to work. I felt like crying, but I didn't. One more hour and it was time to clock out. I was just finishing putting things away on a shelf when Marianne came over to me again. (207)

"You're to go see the boss right away," she said, nodding in the direction of his office. I had no idea what else there was to talk about, but I went in.

"Elara, please come in. Have a seat," he greeted me again. Then he rummaged in his papers for something and I waited. After a while of searching, he finally found his paper. "Here!" he held the papers out for me and said dryly, "I am so sorry, but I am afraid we are going to have to let you go." He looked at my face. I was stumped and was just about to say something suitable when Hr Hendriks was faster.

"Oh, no. Not what you are thinking. No. Just imagine, I thought about it after our conversation and I remembered another colleague. And he knew someone who happens to work in Ireland. What can I say, they are always looking for people. But you have to decide quickly. I could prepare all papers for you, if you think you can manage to pay them a visit before the end of next week," he said and looked at me questioningly. My eyes started shining and I would have loved to hug him. Of course I didn't do that, but shook his hand instead. I thanked him a thousand times and grinned myself silly. As quickly as possible, I got my shift over with and raced home on my bike. I threw open the door, nearly giving Kyran a heart attack. (208)

"Dear Lord, El, what's going on?" he asked, slightly shocked. I walked over to him and kissed him, then I looked at him, now serious.

"Say, did you really mean it when you asked me to come to Ireland with you? I mean, for real?" I asked.

Kyran looked at me. "Of course I am serious. Not a question. What do you think why I am here?" he asked and took me in his arms. I sat in his lap and looked at him.

"Are you really, really sure?" I asked one more time and tried to fight down a smile. Kyran looked at me, slightly insecure.

"Of course. I want you with me every day, every minute, every second. I don't know why, but when I first saw you, it was like... like, I don't know, magic. It sounds kitsch and I... urgh." Kyran struggled for words, but I took him in my arms and kissed him passionately.

"Alright, it is really just for a short while, but I will stay with you until I have found a place of my own. My company can move me to Dublin. But, as I said, only until I have my own place. We have to take it slow," I told him. Kyran looked at me with stars in his eyes. Then he took me in his arms (209) again and kissed me, and we stayed in each other's arms for a long time.

"Whatever you want," he just said and seemed over the moon.

Chapter Fifteen

After that, everything happened very quickly. I organised my move, and within a few weeks I sat with packed suitcases at Dublin airport. I had shipped all my belongings as freight, which turned out to be less than worth it. I had a total of three boxes. My furniture I had sold without further ado, and those I couldn't get rid of I had thankfully been allowed to store in my neighbour's garage. After all, I didn't know if I wouldn't find my way back some day. Kyran had long since flown ahead and was waiting for me at the airport. He greeted me gushily, while I felt nervous. I was about to start a new life. In three days, I would take on my new job and I was about to start a new life with Kyran.

So here I was with my suitcases, and life raged around me. We drove to his flat in the late afternoon, and Kyran had already freed a corner for me to use. Still somewhat awkwardly I stood there and realized abruptly what was awaiting me. I got dizzy and had to sit down for a moment. Kyran came over immediately and gave me a large sip of whiskey to start with. I quickly downed it in one go. Of course I needed a little time, but I had taken this step and for now there was no going back. I had to let things sink in for   (211) a day before I fully understood that this was reality. Kyran did his best to make me feel as much at home as possible, and I was very thankful for it. He also let me be on the first day and even slept on the sofa. The second day had me feeling a lot better already, and I saw things with new eyes. The days passed in a blink and I started my new job. I enjoyed it and I quickly found a new rhythm.

Well, what can I say, by now I've been here for nearly a year and yes, I still live with Kyran, which does make me proud. We get along better than ever and I don't waste any thought on finding a new flat. Everything is like a dream, and I hope I never wake up.

End